83/9399

As the man turned, slapping the gunny sack into place, Reb saw that he had a broken nose. This must be one of the bank robbers! Reb halted the bay in the road and swung down, sweeping his coat back. The stocky man glanced at him, noted the movement, and did not hesitate a second. He went for his gun and fired as the muzzle cleared leather. The shot spanged into the dirt. He ducked under the horse's neck, fired again, and missed.

Reb went to one knee and fired deliberately. Broken Nose fell on his side, as his face screwed into a mask of pain.

A tall man burst from the door of the store, a gun in his hand. He fired at Reb. The bullet went wide, rapping into a wagon. Then he began to run along the boardwalk, still firing. Reb stretched out his arm and fired once, and the tall man stumbled and went down in a heap. He lay still as the pistol thumped away.

Also by Arthur Moore
Published by Fawcett Books:

THE KID FROM RINCON
TRAIL OF THE GATLINGS
THE STEEL BOX
DEAD OR ALIVE
MURDER ROAD
ACROSS THE RED RIVER
THE HUNTERS
THE OUTLAWS
REBEL

THE GAME OF DEATH

Arthur Moore

ST. ALBERT PUBLIC LIBRARY
5 ST. ANNE STREET
ST. ALBERT, ALBERTA T8N 3Z9

FAWCETT GOLD MEDAL • NEW YORK

Sale of this book without a front cover may be unauthorized. If this book is coverless, it may have been reported to the publisher as "unsold or destroyed" and neither the author nor the publisher may have received payment for it.

A Fawcett Gold Medal Book
Published by Ballantine Books
Copyright © 1993 by Arthur Moore

All rights reserved under International and Pan-American Copyright Conventions. Published in the United States of America by Ballantine Books, a division of Random House, Inc., New York, and simultaneously in Canada by Random House of Canada Limited, Toronto.

Library of Congress Catalog Card Number: 93-90094

ISBN 0-449-14859-9

Manufactured in the United States of America

First Edition: July 1993

1

The dusty, well-rutted stage road climbed the low hill and flowed away into the valley, straight as a Sioux arrow to the town. Rebel paused on the ridge, feeling the bite of the wind, looking around at the vast emptiness of the plains and the distant buildings where smoke rose lazily and disappeared into the haze. Wakefield looked like any other two-bit burg, though it was the largest town in more than a hundred miles in any direction. It sprawled by the listless Hayes River, which wandered from west to east like a lost child.

But the town, as he rode in, was a more extensive place than it had seemed from afar. The main street paralleled the slow-flowing river, most of the stores and saloons on one side, corrals on the other with a few sheds and the livery barn. There were three streets at right angles, crowded with stores, and beyond them a jumble of lanes with houses, shacks, and tents.

The stage road ran north and south, beginning at the railroad town of Ganz Siding; it went north through Carter and Wakefield to Vetter, more than six hundred miles away.

In Wakefield the stage depot was next to the hotel, with the yards and shops across the street, where the blacksmith's hammer could be heard. As he halted by the hotel, Reb glanced along the street to the half-dozen, blue-clad soldiers gathered about the door to the Red Rooster Saloon. They were off duty from Fort Hayes, some twenty miles to the west.

Once, a long time ago, when he was not yet twenty, he'd had troubles with soldiers—troubles started by them—and not a few had vowed to seriously ventilate him. But it had not happened. It was good that these men here did not know about those days or that bluecoats had died in various gunfights with him.

Putting them out of mind, he got down and stood for a few moments, leaning on the bay horse, gazing at the town. The river made a bend here, on flatland, and flowed roughly north and south for a few miles till it took up its eastward journey again across the vast prairie. It was late afternoon and long shadows covered most of the dusty street and the few buildings on the east side.

He wondered if Billy Cook was in town.

He had ridden a far piece to find Billy, who was wanted for a minor crime in Carter. Billy had been slightly tipsy and had shot a bystander while engaged in an altercation with someone else. The plugged bystander was not seriously hurt; the doc thought he might limp a bit when he healed. However, his wife and four children had screamed bloody murder, demanding Billy's head on a pike.

Billy had decamped at once, and the sheriff had been unable to find him, or so he said. Many accused him of not trying very hard. He said he had other more pressing problems than an accidental shooting.

But the merchant's wife posted a reward of fifty dollars for Billy's capture, and about the same time, Rebel received a tip from a saloon hanger-on that Billy had traveled north to Wakefield.

Reb smiled ruefully at the ragged-looking town. Fifty dollars was fifty dollars; it was more than a ranch hand made in a month. And he had no regular job; he had been working for several years as a bounty hunter, with paydays sometimes few and far between, always depending on luck and his prowess. With any luck he'd find Billy in a saloon, collar him, and take him back to Carter and collect the fifty. There was a girl in Carter, Julia, who worked in a millinery shop. He had said hello to her several times, and she had smiled at him, which he thought a good beginning.

"Let's hope Billy's in town," he said to the horse.

Reb was dressed in a leather coat with fringe along the sleeves, a black-checked shirt, and jeans. A cartridge belt wrapped his lean hips, holding the butt-worn .44 that his uncle Isham had given him years ago. About his forehead was a red headband. He owned a hat, but it hung on a cantle string; he wore the hat when it rained. He knew men stared at him, but he paid no attention. He moved through a violent land with the confidence of a jaguar among lessers.

Taking his war bag, Reb went into the hotel and signed for a room.

The county sheriff in Carter had shown him a photograph of Billy Cook, which had been taken in a jailhouse several years past, and Reb had studied it. Billy was a doughface with little pig eyes, a slack mouth, and lank black hair worn long. If a stranger were shown a picture of Billy with those of half a dozen others, and asked to pick out the thief, it was a hundred to one he would pick Billy. He was destined, everyone said, unless he was shot or hanged, to spend most of his life on one work gang or another. No one could recall that he had any good qualities at all . . . or even if *he* knew what they were.

Reb had breakfast next morning in a restaurant a few doors from the hotel. The babble of conversation had died as he entered, and the other customers gazed at him out of the corners of their eyes, noting his self-possession and the .44 on his hip. Even in a frontier town not everyone went armed, and those who did were often lawmen or strangers passing through. Such strangers were frequently quick-triggered and best left alone.

This particular stranger, they noted, was tanned and whipcord lean, with straight brown hair and gray-blue eyes—and a scar on his left cheek. He sat at a table to himself, his back to the wall, and the general conversation in the room gradually returned, somewhat muted. It was a long room with the kitchen at the rear and smelly with lamp oil and grease. The table was covered with an oilcloth speckled with tiny flowers in lined squares.

A slim youngster with a soiled apron tight about his chest brought him a plate of bacon and eggs, and Reb ate slowly and left quietly. The babble increased at once as the door closed behind the stranger. Who the hell was he, anyway? No one knew.

There were nine saloons in town, two of them containing dance halls, and three were little more than deadfalls. Reb started at the south, looking in each one. He found Billy in the fifth, a very ordinary, poorly lighted room with a bar on one side and tables for cardplayers. There was a piano on a raised platform and chairs around it for strummers, but it was too early for them.

It was Billy Doughface all right, without doubt. He looked exactly like his photograph and was hunched over the bar alone, brooding, possibly contemplating his sins . . . or his luck. Men like Billy depended or hoped for a great deal from luck.

The room was very quiet. The single bartender was seated at the far end of the bar, engrossed in a newspaper. He was wearing a yellow-checked vest and had black hair and a full mustache. He did not turn his head when Reb entered. Two customers were huddled over a table near the far wall, under a hanging lamp, with papers between them, doubtless talking some business deal or other. There was no one else in the room.

Reb halted behind the fugitive. "Billy Cook!" he said sharply.

The other's head came up and he paused for a moment, mouth hanging slackly. He was looking into the back-bar mirror. Reb saw something come into the cloudy eyes, then Billy whirled toward him and he caught a glimpse of a shiny metallic object. He kicked Billy's arm, and a shot slammed into the ceiling. In the next instant he wrenched the pistol from Billy and pushed him against the bar.

"You're just as ugly as your picture, Billy."

Doughface growled at him, trying to shake loose. "What you want?"

Reb smiled. "Why, you're worth fifty dollars hard money, Billy. You're going to jail."

Billy swore, and Reb turned him about quickly, forcing him forward over the bar. "Put your hands behind you."

"Lemme go, dammit!"

"Put 'em behind you or I'll pull your ears off."

Grumpily, Billy did as he was ordered, and Reb deftly bound his hands with a length of stout cord. Billy was wearing an old rusty coat and jeans. He had on a smelly checked shirt with the makin's in one pocket. There was a sheathed knife on his belt, which Reb removed.

As he did so, one of the two men at the table came across the room. He was an older man and wore a circle-star badge on his coat. Engraved on it were two words: WAKEFIELD at the top, and MARSHAL at the bottom. He had a rather square face with a gray mustache and bright blue eyes under a black hat brim. "What's this?" he asked.

Reb nodded to him. "Hello, Marshal. This man is Billy Cook, wanted in Carter for shooting a citizen. I'm taking him in for the reward."

The marshal looked hard at Billy. "Izzat so . . . He can't be worth much."

"Fifty dollars."

"My name ain't Billy What's-his-name," Billy said in a whining voice. "I never shot nobody."

"He's also a liar," Reb said, "and probably a lot of things we don't know about yet." He cocked his head. "Ugly sonofabitch, isn't he?"

"Not too pretty," the marshal agreed.

"D'you mind if I hold him in your lockup till morning? It's a three-day ride to Carter."

"No. Bring him along." The lawman headed for the door. "We got plenty room." He paused on the boardwalk. "Best see if he got any money on him. Otherwise he might go hungry."

"Goddammit!" Billy yelled. "You put me in jail, you got to feed me!"

"He's been in plenty jails. I guess some of them fed him."

The marshal nodded gravely. "We'll find some scraps for him. Come on."

His office was on the first side street; a smallish, square room with two ancient desks, a rack of rifles on the wall behind them, a clutter of posters on the other walls, and a small blackbelly stove. A sign on the window read: WM T. WINTERS, MARSHAL.

Inside, at the smaller of the two desks, a young man in a blue shirt and jeans was writing in a ledger. He was lean and tanned and had curls of black hair on his forehead. He wore the same star badge and jumped up as they entered. "G'morning, Marshal."

"Mornin' Jim." The marshal pointed to Billy. "Untie 'im and put 'im in a cage for the night."

The deputy hustled the protesting Billy through a heavy door into the back, and Reb heard a jail door clang. Winters lowered himself into a chair behind the large desk and pushed his hat back. His weathered face was deeply lined and his jaw stubbled. "This here's a quiet town mostly. Your frien's the first one we had in the calaboose in three days. You from Carter, huh?"

"I travel a bit," Reb said. "Got to in my trade."

"Yeh, 'spect you do." The marshal fished in a drawer and brought out a sheaf of wanted dodgers. "Billy Cook—Billy Cook—that name sounds familiar. I seem t'remember something about him." He thumbed through the flyers and smiled. "Yeah—here it is. You're in luck, Mister— What is your name anyways?"

"Wiley. Folks calls me Reb."

"Well, that no-account *is* your prisoner." He passed the poster across. "You got a hunnerd more comin' to you. Billy's been stealin' cows."

The Wakefield weekly, called the *Democrat*, was just out. It was a two-sheet, eight-page edition, and Reb bought a copy and read it in his room. A great part of one page was devoted to the recent murders of two prominent local men. The murders were described as mysteries. The culprit or culprits had not been found or named.

One victim was Homer Chartis, owner of the largest merchantile establishment in the territory; the other his general manager, Joseph Aiken. They had been shot to death within days of each other. The undertaker was certain the weapon used was the same in both cases, and the shootings were identical; one shot in the back of the head for each. The shooter had stood directly behind each man and fired at point-blank range; impossible to miss.

Marshal Winters had no suspects in custody and none in mind. In an editorial, the newspaper editor was of the opinion that the murders would go unsolved. He stressed the mystery aspect, a highly unusual occurrence in the territory. Most shootings were direct, out in the open or across a gaming table. These two murders smacked of jealousy or revenge or something deeper. What terrible secret linked the two victims?

It set all tongues a-wagging. A reward of fifteen hundred dollars was offered by Mrs. Chartis for information leading to the arrest and conviction of the killer of her husband and his manager.

A good many solutions had been offered him, Winters said, but none had led to anything. He suspected the motive was probably robbery, since each man had been killed in his office and the office ransacked. But he had no clues.

"No tellin' what the killer found," he said to Reb. "The petty cash box was empty, no money on either man or anywhere in the offices. They was gunned down in closed rooms. Nobody heard nothing."

But was robbery the motive for the shootings? The editor wondered why a robber would kill the two men.

"And," Winters said to Reb, "the shootings were planned ahead of time. The killer brought along a cushion—not like none of them found in the store. He fired through the cushion to help deaden the sounds.''

Reb nodded. ''Premeditated.''

''That's what I said,'' Winters agreed.

2

The posted reward was large enough to be tempting, and Reb thought about it for several days. He had been living on the money from bounties, which were seldom as high as five hundred dollars, and had put aside very little. When he had it, he sent money to a bank in St. Louis, but the total in his account was less than three hundred dollars. If he could manage to collect the fifteen hundred offered in Wakefield, he might settle down and start a business—or even go on to school. The thought had crossed his mind that he might become a lawyer.

He wondered at Marshall Winters's feelings. Possibly, the marshal might not welcome a stranger poking into his bailiwick. Few lawmen would; they were often jealous creatures, and considered bounty hunters to be amateurs. Many lawmen refused to deal with them and would order them to hit the road.

It might turn out to be an impossible situation.

Reb decided to return to Carter at once with his prisoner and collect his money. He would leave in the morning and a few days later would see Julia again. That thought made him smile.

He had supper in a restaurant, beef and potatoes, and stopped in a saloon on the way back to the hotel to have a beer. Someone had left a deck of cards on a table, so he sat down and laid out a game of solitaire. He was placing the queen on a king when Marshal Winters entered, looked about the room, and approached the table.

"You-all mind if I set down?"

"Help yourself, Marshal." Reb swept up the cards and stacked them neatly. "You feed my prisoner?"

"Jim give him something. I dunno what the hell it was." Winters took off his hat and ruffled his gray hair. "I seen what you did, taking Billy Cook's gun away from him."

Reb grinned. "I had to. He woulda shot me."

The marshal nodded. "What I'm saying is, some would have shot him with his own iron."

"I hate to shoot a man because of fifty dollars."

"Well, I seen it happen over a lot less." Winters found a cigar in his vest pocket and looked at it critically. "You live in Carter?"

"I don't live anywhere in particular. I have to go where the warrants lead me."

The older man nodded again and put his hat on. "Yes, I 'spect you do." He squinted at Reb. "I never tried that bounty dodge to make a livin'. Maybe because I got married too soon. Purty much had to stay in one place—after the war, that was." He searched his pockets for a match. "You like that kinda life, do you?"

"Well, I can be my own boss. That's important to me. Come and go as I please."

"Then you ain't married?"

"No." Reb smiled. "I doubt if any woman would put up with me, ramming around the country all the time, never in one place very long." He thought, with a twinge, of Julia in Carter. It would probably be the same with her.

Marshal Winters puffed on the cigar and looked critically at the ash. "I been getting pushed on this here Chartis-Aiken shooting. Folks think I ain't doing nothing." He sighed deeply. "Not a hell of a lot to do . . ."

Reb said, "The killer might have been somebody passing through, and he's long gone."

"Yeah, there's that."

"You don't think so?"

Winters puffed the cigar. "I don't mind him being somebody passin' through, but how did this feller know how to get into the store and out without being seen—and why'd he shoot them two? He had to know too much to be a stranger."

"Ummm."

"The reward is fifteen hunnerd—and might go higher." Winters squinted at Reb. "That interest you?"

"Of course it does." Reb sipped beer and nodded. "But I know how you lawmen feel about—"

"Lissen, son. I'm an old man, and them things don't worry me none. I got a gut feelin' this killer is laughin' at me. He knows I ain't going to catch him." He pointed with the cigar. "But you might."

Reb was mildly surprised. He said nothing for a moment. "Then you think he might still be in town?"

"He might be. You read the papers—what if it wasn't robbery? What if the bodies was robbed to cover up the real reason?"

"Yes, that's possible. . . ."

"Fifteen hunnerd is a lot of money."

Reb smiled. "You've got a deputy."

Winters shook his head. "Jim is a part-time deputy is all. He ain't trained in police work, and to tell the goddamn truth, neither am I. I just got elected to keep the peace. This killer has got a damn good chance of gettin' away with it." He let out his breath slowly. "And I'll lose the next election."

Reb fiddled with the deck of cards. Fifteen hundred dollars was a pile of money! It would be nice to lean against it one winter's day, not having to go out in a storm looking for someone whose face was on a poster.

His head jerked up as they heard the shot.

It had sounded a long way off, but Winters swore and pushed out of his chair. "Some damn drunk, prob'ly, shootin' at the moon. I better go see. . . ." He hurried out.

Reb followed him to the boardwalk and watched the other stride away into the dark. It was a starry night with no wind. No one else seemed interested in the shot; they were not all that rare. The marshal was doubtless right, a drunk shooting at the sky. But why only one shot? Most drunks would empty their revolvers.

He shrugged and went up to bed.

But it was a different story in the morning.

The town's only bank had been robbed the night before.

The hotel clerk told him the news, and Reb walked to the jail office to talk to Winters. The deputy, Jim, was in the street organizing a posse of eager young men to go after the robbers. They milled about, shouting and laughing, raising dust, till the marshal walked out and yelled at them to get the hell away.

Apparently, no one had seen the robbers leave the bank, so it was not known where they'd gone. Jim had decided to try the Vetter road north, and the posse galloped off in that direction.

Winters went back inside and plopped in his chair. "They all on a wild-goose chase, lettin' off steam."

Reb sat opposite. "How did it happen?"

Winters took off his hat and scratched his gray head. "Two men went to Tim Feeny's house last night—Tim, he owns the bank. They took him and his wife to the bank and made Feeny open the safe. Then they tied 'em both up, grabbed the stuff, and skedaddled."

"Were the two hurt?"

"Not exactly. Well, Tim, he had a bad case of the upsets. Heart poundin'—scared him and the missus half to death. Anxious attack, the doc called it. Tim is home in bed now."

"There was a shot. We both heard it."

The older man nodded. "Miz Feeny, she's small-boned. Little tiny thing. Them robbers was in a big hurry and didn't tie her up good. She was able to skin out'n the ropes. She freed Tim, and he staggered outside and fired into the air. Then he collapsed."

"And no one saw them go."

"That's right. They coulda gone any direction. Jim's got a wild hair, going up toward Vetter."

"There were only two men?"

"Yeah. The Feenys are sure of that. Only two. I got a description of them."

"How much money did they get?"

The marshal put his hat back on. "I talked to Mr. Dolan, the manager, this morning. They cleaned out the safe. He thinks about nine, ten thousand. He's figgering it up now."

Reb shook his head sadly. "Is Mr. Feeny going to live?"

"The doc thinks he will. He's calmed down some already. His missus is taking good care of him. This is the second time he's been robbed." The marshal looked in a desk drawer for a cigar. "How d'you like that dodge of robbin' a bank at night?"

"Not bad. It means few witnesses if they do it right, and I guess they did. But one thing—they had to know where Mr. Feeny lived."

Winters found the cigar and rolled it in his stubby fingers. "I 'spect they did some homework. There's strangers in town all the time, of course. These fellers must have hung around and maybe followed Feeny home. They seen how the bank operated."

"Yes, I expect so. So what's next, Marshal?"

"I was fixin' to ask you that."

Reb smiled. "Is there a reward?"

Winters lit the cigar and puffed blue smoke toward the ceiling. "You like bein' in the reward business . . . ?"

"Have to be. I don't have a big-paying job with the city."

"Big-paying job?"

Reb chuckled. "Let's say, regular-paying job."

"Yeah. Let's us say that. I dunno about a reward. You go ask Dolan."

A dusty and tired posse returned at dusk the same day. They had ridden about a dozen miles north and found no tracks of two horsemen on the road.

Deputy Jim asked, "What you want us t'do now, Marshal? We guessed wrong."

"Go on home," Winters said. "Them two, they in St. Louie by now."

John Dolan, bank manager, had been a banker all his adult life and had never before been involved in a robbery. It had given him a case of the shakes. He hadn't exactly been involved personally—the robbers hadn't entered with guns during business hours—but the bank had been the victim, as well as Mr. Feeny. It brought it all close.

He was forty-four, and very neat. Those under him said "fussy." Dolan prided himself on being neat and presentable. He wore thick spectacles that enlarged his brown eyes, and no one had ever seen him in anything but a store suit, buttoned up properly. He was generally disliked by the help, though he did not know it. His wife disliked many of his traits, too, and wondered how she hadn't noticed them before they'd been married. She often shouted at him in frustration. Dolan never understood that at all.

He was alarmed to see the big man in a fringed leather coat and red headband, a revolver at his hip, walk into the office without being announced. To Dolan he looked like one of the wild trappers or frontier scouts who sometimes were seen in town, often hanging around a saloon, loud and ribald. Dolan slid down a bit in his chair and hunched his narrow shoulders, staring.

His visitor said, "My name is Wiley, Mr. Dolan. I came to ask you about the robbery."

He had a soft, almost gentle voice, nonthreatening. He sat in a chair opposite the desk and even smiled.

Dolan found his voice after a few throat-clearings. "Y-Yes. What about it?"

"Are you offering a reward, sir?"

Jesus! The man seemed to fill the office. Dolan took a long breath and gripped the arms of the chair. "Yes. Th-There will be a reward. We want our money back."

"Don't you care about the robbers?"

Dolan sat up a little. This big man seemed to be on the side of the law. Dolan's confidence was returning by dribs and drabs. "We'd like to s-see them prosecuted, yes. But we want the money back." He felt his heart thumping less hard. This stranger was not going to skin him. "It's d-depositors' money, you know."

The big man said, "What can you tell me about it?"

"The robbery?" Dolan picked papers off the desk and laid them down again. He straightened an inkwell. "I—I guess you know about them bringing Mr. Feeny and his wife here?"

"Yes."

"Apparently no one saw them. It was late."

"I heard the shot about ten o'clock. I was with Marshal Winters at the time."

"Um. Oh. Did you . . . Well, nine o'clock is late for Wakefield, of course." Dolan fussed with a pen. "The two forced Mr. Feeny to open the safe, then they took everything in it." He put the pen down, lined up with the blotter, and picked up a pencil. "It was lucky for them—and unlucky at the same time."

"What do you mean?"

Dolan managed a smile that twisted his face. "I mean that Mr. Feeny had been robbed before—some while ago in another place. That was before I went to work for him. But now we have two safes here in the bank. One is out in the open, the other is concealed. The robbers didn't know about the second safe."

Reb nodded approvingly. "Very smart. But if you lost ten thousand—"

"Yes, unfortunately there was too much in that safe overnight. There should not have been." The bank manager sighed. "One gets complacent. It's our only excuse."

"Can you tell me, how long was it from the time the robbers left the bank before Mr. Feeny fired the shot?"

"Mrs. Feeny guessed it to be about twenty minutes." He stressed the word *guessed*. "He fired the shot and collapsed. They found him in the street with Mrs. Feeny moaning over him. So of course neither can say which way the robbers went. Have you talked to her?"

"Not yet."

Dolan shook his head, took off his thick glasses and rubbed his eyes. "There are four roads out of town. It's anyone's guess which one they took."

Reb rose. "Thanks, Mr. Dolan."

"I hope you get our money back—you're going after them?"

Reb smiled. "What will the reward be?"

"At least five hundred . . . It'll be posted by nightfall."

Reb paused in front of the bank building. Four roads out of town . . . But the men could easily have gone across country. Wagons followed roads, but horsemen could go as they pleased. Or they might have stayed in town, in a previously arranged hideout. They had proved themselves inventive, after all.

In the hotel stable he saddled the bay horse and rode to the river, thinking about the reward. Five hundred was a lot of money; Marshal Winters and his part-time deputy weren't going to collect it.

What if he went after it? He could leave Billy Cook in the calaboose for as long as it would take. Billy wouldn't like it, but who cared what Billy liked?

The river flowed serenely along, lined with willows and flickering cottonwoods. He rode along it for a short space and found two young boys fishing from a high bank. He asked them how deep the water was.

One said, "Purty deep right here, but not nowhere else except in pools."

Reb asked, "Could anyone go downstream in a boat?"

They both laughed and shook heads. "Water's mostly a couple inches deep. There ain't any boats anyhow."

"None at all?"

"Nope. Not on this here stream."

Reb waved to them and turned the horse. He knew that travelers called the Platte River a mile wide and an inch deep. This Hayes River was apparently the same, except of course in winter's floods. But it was certain the robbers had not gotten away in a boat.

In town he inquired the way and was directed to the Feeny home. It was a stone and clapboard house well kept up, the boards painted white, the chimney of gray fieldstone. It was hedged in with shrubs and plants in front, and had a row of red flowerpots along the wide veranda railing. One of the Feenys was fond of plants. He could see part of a stable building in the rear where a young man was brushing down a sorrel house.

Dismounting, Reb walked to the front door and rapped. It was opened by a slight woman in a dark dress; she looked very fragile, with tightly drawn features. She stared at him in surprise, her head far back. "What d'you want?"

"Are you Mrs. Feeny?"

"Yes . . ."

Reb said softly, "I'm going after the men who robbed you, Mrs. Feeny. May I ask you a few questions?"

She hesitated, looking behind him, biting her lower lip. "You're working with Marshal Winters?"

"Yes, I am—in a way."

She blinked at him, then made up her mind. "Very well." She stood aside and let him in. "Come into the parlor. Mr. Feeny is asleep right now. The doctor gave him something to make him rest. What is your name, young man?"

"Reb Wiley, ma'am. Will your husband recover all right?"

"The doctor was here this morning, yes. He says my husband's heart is fine. He just needs rest."

"I'm glad to hear it." The parlor was a square room with heavy, dark furniture that looked able to withstand cannon fire. It would probably take two men to lift one of the chairs. There was a thick-legged table in the center of the room holding a clutter of gold-framed pictures and a ceramic lamp. The walls were busy with flowered paper.

Reb lowered himself into a chair so he wouldn't tower over her. "What can you tell me about the two men, Mrs. Feeny? Did they call each other by name?"

She pulled back a heavy drape and sunlight flooded in. She rounded the table and sat, facing him, fiddling with a pink cameo brooch at her throat. She frowned, looking past him. "One was tall, the other much shorter, only an inch or two taller than I am, but rather heavyset. The short one did all the talking, and I'm sure he called the other one Dave."

"Dave."

"Yes. The tall one never opened his mouth that I recall."

"You heard no last name?"

"No, only Dave. He said it once. As a matter of fact he talked very softly. It was more frightening than if he'd yelled at us."

"Did you notice anything at all out of the ordinary about either of them?"

She pursed thin lips. "They were dressed like anyone else, but the short one had a broken nose. I mean it had been broken a time ago, as if he'd been one of those saloon fighters. I read about them in the paper."

"What about an accent?"

"No. I don't think so."

"Any scars or tattoos you could see?"

"No . . ."

"Did the short one threaten you and your husband?"

"Oh yes! He said he'd kill us if we didn't do exactly as he ordered." She fingered her chin nervously. "The tall one had blondish hair. I remember thinking it was about the same shade as our daughter's. The short one was dark."

"Good. Anything else you recall?"

"Well, what worried Tim most of all—my husband, I mean—was that they'd find out about the other safe and shoot us because we didn't tell them."

"Yes, a very real worry. It was good they didn't find out. Of course, at the time you couldn't know how much they knew."

She smiled. "Yes, exactly! Especially since they had known where we live."

"Is there anything else you can tell me, Mrs. Feeny?"

She thought for a few moments, head down, looking at the carpeted floor, a cambric handkerchief knotted in her hand. "I—I don't think so. . . ."

Reb got up and went to the door. "You've been a very great help, Mrs. Feeny. I hope your husband is better soon."

"Thank you . . ."

3

Town marshal Winters had no possibility of arresting the two men who had robbed the bank. If he and a posse had chased them at once, when they had departed with the loot, he would have had the right to pursue them to the Pacific Ocean—and as far out as he could swim.

But he had not. In fact his jurisdiction ended at the edge of town. Of course, no one minded if he stretched it a few miles to bring in a culprit—or whomever. But to go after the two was impossible, because of his age and condition, if nothing else. He was long in the tooth, and his daughter would probably never speak to him again if he even contemplated such an action. She had been urging him to hang up his badge when he reached fifty, three years past. He could go into some quiet business and, with all the friends he had made, would certainly make his beans and put a little by.

However, Wakefield was generally a quiet place, not like some of the raucous end-of-trail cow towns farther south. Keeping the peace was not a chore. When a bit of lawlessness occurred, like the bank robbery, he sent the details by stagecoach to lawmen north and south of the town. The nearest telegraph line was at Ganz Siding, hundreds of miles south, at the railroad. If an outlaw could outrun the law, he was safe.

Unless someone like Reb Wiley took out after him.

Winters had been mightily impressed with the young bounty hunter the moment he'd first seen him in the saloon with Billy Cook. Billy might have killed most men—he'd been quick as greased lightning. But Reb had been quicker and had taken Billy's gun away with apparent ease.

Billy had then made no further trouble, not even complaining about the jailhouse food.

Reb did not swagger, Winters thought, as he'd seen well-known gunmen do. Eastern writers made some gunslingers famous, men who played cards for a living and hung around train depots with six-guns and bowie knives in plain view, for tourists to gawk at.

But Reb had a natural, catlike grace and coordination. He'd watched Reb enter a saloon room, ignoring the stares, and superbly confident, so that men slid aside for him, while Reb, at the same time, noted everyone and everything about him.

Winters smiled to himself, thinking that if the two robbers met Reb, they would be well-advised to hand over their weapons and the money and go along quietly. Reb had a presence that seemed actually tangible at times. Marshal Winters had witnessed dozens of fights and shootings in his day as a lawman, but he'd never seen anyone like Reb.

He had to stop himself and swear under his breath. He was beginning to feel sorry for the two robbers!

Reb walked the bay horse out of town, heading west along the road that led to Elland, far off beyond the hills, well past Fort Hayes. The land was undulating prairie, with the river south of him unseen in the haze. After a few miles he left the road, turning north, moving slowly, looking for tracks.

He made a wide circle, crossed the Vetter stage road and continued eastward for miles, moving and stopping, moving and stopping, eyes on the ground.

When he found tracks, he swung down and examined them; they were fresh. Two horses moving at a walk, pointing northwest. Who else but the robbers? They would be walking the horses at night, and they would not expect pursuit—who knew where they had gone? In a few days the tracks would be erased by the wind and sun, a fragile tie to their crime.

Reb climbed back on the bay. The prairie was giving way to desert, and the tracks were very plain, easy to follow. No attempt had been made to hide them. He moved faster.

By nightfall he judged himself to be about fifteen miles north of Wakefield. Were the two robbers heading for Vetter? It was a town probably three hundred miles north, and large enough to be called a city. It would certainly be a riotous place for two thieves to spend their gold.

And there was nothing, as far as he knew, between Wakefield and Vetter but hills and salt flats, coyotes and snakes. Could he catch up to them?

He camped in a hollow, and in the morning found the remains of a campfire not a mile off, where the two had stopped. But the embers were cold. They were well ahead of him and doubtless not in a hurry. He could imagine them telling each other endless stories about how they intended to spend the money. Ten thousand dollars was an enormous amount! An ordinary family could live for years and years on it.

Late in the afternoon, he came to a huge, dry lakebed and halted. It was flat as a billiard table in the fading light, and went on into the hazy, indefinite horizon. The tracks led straight into it and were as plain as if etched by a plow.

Reb considered. In daylight, on that flat lake-that-once-was, he could be seen for miles. He assumed the pursued were a day's ride ahead of him, but there was always the possibility they were not. Maybe they had stopped and had spotted him following. If they had, they would ambush him.

There was a moon, providing almost no light. But he could make out the tracks, much darker traces than the dried mud. He followed for hours, walking the horse.

When it began to get light, he halted again. The tracks were curving away toward the west, and as dawn brightened into day, he could make out the sketchy blue hills in the distance. Would they wait for him in the foothills?

He had to chance it and continue. The sun would soon make it very hot for him on the flats—and it did. He reached the hills by late afternoon and no one fired at him. The tracks led directly into the hills, but before dark he found the remains of another campfire and put his hand into the ashes. Warm! He was not far behind.

In a coulee, Reb dug a pit and made a hidden fire to broil meat and heat coffee. Then he covered the fire with dirt and rolled in his blankets. He knew only what Mrs. Feeny had told him of the two men, the tall and the short, but they had been somewhat clever so far, and he'd be careful. When he caught up with them, they might still have a few tricks up their sleeves.

And they were two to his one. However, he had one high card. They did not know him, either.

In the morning he discovered he had camped within several miles of a shacky settlement. It was a ragged, half-mile-long cluster of buildings that ranged along the steep side of a narrow canyon where a silver stream trickled.

It was a mining camp, all the buildings on one side of the stream, and it called itself Huntling.

He had not known it was there; the map did not show it. It was obviously one of those temporary settlements that sprang up about a mining strike. The town would fade away when the lode played out; the shacks would weather and rot and eventually only bricks and bits of mortared stone and heaps of trash would remain, along with the deep holes in hillsides.

The rounded hills about the settlement were barren and bleak, and a cold wind seemed to live in the narrow valley. But no sensible person would—unless attracted mightily. By gold. Gold, the great leveler.

Reb entered the canyon at the east end, where a few tents had been erected by the creek. There was a road of sorts, deeply rutted by wagon wheels, and it looked as temporary a place as he had ever seen. It was a cool morning, and there were few persons to be seen; a man chopping wood gave him a quick glance, and another, toting water from the stream, nodded to him. Everyone was busy at something; a few washed clothes in the icy water, smoke poured from tin chimneys, so others were cooking or heating the huts. One man by the road was pounding at a slab-sided shack. He wore a linsey-woolsey shirt and old army pants stuffed into boots. Reb paused and asked him if there was any law in the town.

The man stared at him. "Hell, mister, there ain't any law closer'n Kansas City!" He shrugged. " 'Ceptin' Colonel Colt."

The road was anything but straight; it curved and twisted, following the contours of the hill. In the center of the makeshift settlement was the largest and best-looking building. It was actually two stories high, and had once been whitewashed, at least in front, and had a long veranda porch facing the road, not connected to the buildings on either side. It had a dozen steps up from the road, and over the wide door was a yellow-on-black sign: SALOON *Jerry Wilde, prop.*

As Reb neared the steps, he heard shots from inside, and in a few moments two men wearing white aprons dragged a body through the swinging doors and left it on the porch, one arm flopping down the steps. One of the men walked to the far end of the porch and yelled for Benny to go get Doc Summers. Then both went back inside.

Reb swung down, flipped the reins around the hitch rack, and mounted the steps. Several men came from the saloon and turned the deceased over, muttering about him to each other. The departed looked like an ordinary miner—with a bloody hole in his chest. A pistol was still in his belt. Evidently he'd suffered from a case of the slows. Reb went by them and entered the saloon.

Inside, the big room was quiet, with a faint smell of gunpowder lingering in the still air. Reb asked for beer at the long bar. "What happened?"

A mustached barman made a face. "Some gent accused the wrong hombre of cheatin'." He nodded toward a table, and Reb turned to see a black-clad gambler laying out cards as if nothing had occurred.

The bartender set a glass before him, and Reb asked, "You get many strangers in town?"

The other looked at him as if for the first time. "They comes and they goes. You a lawman?"

"No, I'm not. But I'm looking for two friends, one short and one tall, traveling together. The short one has a broken nose." Reb sipped the beer and studied the man behind the bar.

The other's eyes went to the door, down to the bar, and back to Reb. He shook his dark head. "Haven't seen 'em." He moved away, mopping the bar.

Reb smiled at the man's back. So he *had* seen the two. Probably the bartender did not believe that he was not a lawman—he was obviously not a miner. Certainly other deputies and sheriffs had come into the settlement seeking wanted men. Probably they were not welcome.

Finishing the beer, Reb decided to poke into the rest of the settlement; the chances were good that the two robbers were still in the place—if they had no idea they had been followed. Owlhoots were always eager to spend money when they had it. This was an opportunity. Easy come, easy go.

As he turned toward the door, a well-dressed, middle-aged man came along the bar, smiling, and stopped by him. "Good day, friend. I'm Jerry Wilde."

Reb nodded politely. Wilde was a dapper little man with a carefully waxed mustache and fussily groomed, wavy, graying hair. His cravat was immaculate, and his tailored suit fit perfectly, dark gray and hardly wrinkled. There were rings on his fingers; he might have stepped out of a band box moments ago.

Wilde said, "I did not mean to eavesdrop, sir, but I could not help hearing your conversation with Dan." He indicated the barman. "I would only caution you, sir, if you *are* a lawman, that this town unfortunately does not take kindly to them. I must say it is a position I do not subscribe to. We should have law here . . . and we will, in time."

Reb said quietly, "I told him the truth. I am not a lawman."

"Then perhaps a bounty brings you here?" Wilde shook his head sadly. "I deplore violence—such as occurred here shortly ago, but I am usually powerless to prevent it. That, sir, is the reason I am speaking to you."

Reb smiled. "Thanks for the warning."

"Not at all." The little man turned his head slightly, then looked back at Reb and lowered his voice. "The men you seek were here last evening." He gave a little bow and walked away.

Reb went out to the wide veranda and stood, looking at the dozen or so buildings he could see as the road turned. So they had been here, last evening. Where had they spent the night? Did they know someone who put them up? Probably his best bet would be to wait, look, and listen, make sure they were not in any of the deadfalls, and hope they would turn up, hoping as well they hadn't hit the trail this morning, moving out as he came in.

He frowned at the shacks. The lumber, most used and old, had been hauled in, probably over a period of time, and the town hammered together. The buildings looked as if a good stiff wind would blow them into rubble. They were all ugly and unpainted, set down every which-away. The road wandered as if laid out by a drunk, no two buildings in a line. The air was still, and the thick smoke from dozens of chimneys and open fires hung over the squeezed-in valley like a pall. It tickled his nose as he went down the steps to the bay horse.

He untied the reins and leaned against the animal, holding onto the horn. Not much to go on, two men, one tall and one short, with a broken nose. He would probably be lucky to see them together. He wished he knew more about them. More than just the name Dave.

A group of blue-clad cavalrymen came along the road toward him in single file, walking the horses. They were led by a grizzled sergeant; all slouched in the saddles, most unshaven, yellow stripes down their legs into the dusty leggin's. The tough-looking sergeant, on a sorrel horse, looked hard at Reb as he went past.

Reb watched them narrowly. They reminded him of other soldiers, years ago in Rustin, where he'd been born and grew up. Soldiers who had tried their best to kill him. The feud had started over a minor slight, and only ended when a number of bluecoats were dead or disabled. None of them could believe Reb's uncanny ability with a six-gun. Not from one so young.

The troopers passed by and disappeared. Reb mounted the bay and rode along the winding road in the opposite direction. Nearly all the shacks were on the upper side, and were living quarters for the most part. He saw no hotel at all; there was a general merchandise store, a stable, and a blacksmith shop. As he went by, the blacksmith, a big man in a leather apron, was arguing with two men over a wagon wheel.

There were hitching poles in front of the general store, and several horses waiting three-legged. As Reb approached, a man came from the store with a heavy gunnysack and began to tie it on behind the cantle of one of the saddles. He was short and thick-chested, wearing a long rusty-black coat and a black hat that had seen many winters.

As he turned, slapping the sack into place, Reb saw he had a nose that had been broken some time in the past and poorly set. This must be one of them!

Reb halted the bay in the road and swung down, sweeping his coat back. The stocky man glanced at him, noted the movement, and did not hesitate an instant. He went for his gun and fired as the muzzle cleared leather. The shot spanged into the dirt. He ducked under the horse's neck and fired again, the shot smashing into a wall across the road.

Reb went to one knee and fired deliberately. The other's pistol flipped away, and Broken Nose fell on his side, holding one arm as his face screwed into a mask of pain.

A tall man burst from the door of the store, a gun in his hand. He fired at Reb. The bullet went wide, rapping into a wagon on the road. Then, unaccountably, he began to run along the boardwalk, still firing. Reb stretched out his arm and fired once, and the tall man stumbled and went down in a heap. He lay still as the pistol thumped away.

4

The fight had taken only seconds. Reb picked up the stocky man's gun and frowned at him. The bullet had gone through the right hand. Broken Nose was trying to wrap his wipe about it, gritting his teeth and glaring at Reb. "Who the hell're you?"

Reb ignored him. The store owner, in a long apron, with several others craning their necks behind him, was standing in the doorway. Reb asked, "Is there a doctor in town?"

"They's only Doc Summers. He's the undertaker, but he had some schoolin'. He fixes broken bones and the like." He turned. "You, Harry, go get the doc."

To the wounded man, Reb said, "What's your name?"

"Go to hell."

"You want the doctor to treat that hand or not? If not, you'll probably lose the arm by the time we get back to Wakefield."

The man continued to glare at him, and from him to the huddled form on the boardwalk. He mumbled something under his breath.

A bystander turned the tall man's body over. "This one's deader'n a rock."

Reb said, "See if there's anything on him to tell his name." He reloaded the .44 as he watched the man search the body and turn up a worn leather wallet. The searcher looked into it and nodded to Reb.

"His name was David Hinks." In the next moment he said, "Jesus Christ!"

Reb went to him. "What is it?"

The man held up a sheaf of greenbacks. "Lookit the money! They must be hunnerds here!"

"It belongs to the bank in Wakefield," Reb said, taking it. "These two held it up a few days ago. Anything else on him?"

"Nothing. Pocketknife, tobacco . . . that's all."

There were fat saddlebags on the horse next to the one with the gunnysack. Reb unfastened the flaps and looked inside. Money! The bank's money, still in wrappers. They hadn't had a chance to spend much.

The undertaker, Doc Summers, appeared. He was a lanky forty-year-old with a drooping black mustache and a long, sad face. He wore a black frock coat that had seen better days, scuffed boots, and a tall, rusty hat. He examined Hinks quickly, shook his head, "He's gone."

He looked at the other's hand. "Bad. Damn bad. It hurts like hell, huh?"

Reb said again to Broken Nose. "What's your name?"

"Go to hell, lawman."

Reb smiled at the skinny undertaker. "That's all, Doctor. He doesn't need the hand treated."

Summers stared at him in astonishment. "But he'll lose it! All them jagged little bones festering . . ."

"Yeah, that's a shame." Reb motioned to Broken Nose. "Climb on your horse. We're leaving."

The man glared at him and took a long breath, sighing and grinding his teeth. "Name's Bob Bassett."

Reb smiled. "I like cooperative prisoners. We'll treat the hand, Doctor."

"We'll have to go back to my office. I didn't bring nothing with me." Summers had come in a buckboard, having heard the shooting. From long experience, he expected a body.

He and several others lifted the departed into the wagon bed, and Reb tied the two horses on behind. He pointed to the wagon seat, and Bassett climbed up, wincing.

Reb followed the buckboard down the road to Summers's place of business, a wide shack with two doors, one wide enough for the wagon. It had a sign: F. R. SUMMERS UNDERTAKING. Under it a smaller sign read: FURNITURE MADE TO ORDER.

The building had four rooms. There was a tiny front office with a worn desk and lantern, and a larger back room with two metal-topped tables. The body of the miner from Wilde's saloon lay on one, covered with a sheet. There were newly made coffins stacked along one wall. In the back was a carpenter's shop where a man was sawing wood. The fourth room was Summers's living quarters.

They lifted the body out of the wagon and laid it on the other table. Summers quickly went through the pockets. "Not a penny on him."

Reb said, "There's his horse and saddle. It's yours. Bury him deep. He won't need a headboard unless you want to give him one. Nobody cares about him."

Summers nodded and turned to Bassett. "Let's see that wound." He unwound the wipe, examined the hand under a hanging lamp and clucked his tongue. "There's some laudanum here. . . ." He fussed in a cabinet and came back with a bottle, handing it to Bassett. "Drink this."

He worked over the wound for half an hour as Bassett groaned and swore, then Summers bandaged it carefully. "You go see a real doctor soon's you get to Wakefield. You're never gonna use that hand like you did before. . . ." He rigged a sling around Bassett's shoulder and laid the arm in it. "Carry it like that."

The hurt man's face was drawn and strained; it must pain him like blue blazes, Reb reflected, despite the medicine. He protested mightily when Reb said they were leaving at once for Wakefield.

"Nothing to stay here for," Reb said. "Get on your horse."

They rode out slowly and left the settlement behind, heading west to gain the Vetter road. There was no sense in crossing the dry lake again. The robbers had done it to evade pursuit, to keep from encountering travelers and the way stations. He had no such worry.

Bassett was quiet, hugging his hurt hand and muttering to himself; he was doubtless cursing his luck. Summers's prediction that he would never use the hand as he once had was probably on his mind.

They reached the road before dark, crossed it and camped well away from it, in a clump of trees. When he slid down from the horse, Bassett sat hunched over, swearing. He growled. "Is they a doc in Wakefield?"

"I think so. . . ."

They made a supper of beans and coffee, then Reb said, "Put your feet out."

"What?"

"You heard me."

"What for?"

"I'm going to tie them." He showed the other a length of stout cord.

Bassett was surprised. "You figger me to run off?"

"Shut up and put your feet out."

"Damn you! You shoot me and now you gonna tie me like a goddamn heifer!"

"Yes, I am."

Bassett groaned, but he had to comply. His feet were tied securely, and he knew he could never untie them with only one hand. He was not used to obeying orders, but it was increasingly apparent he had no choice. This man meant what he said.

In the morning they took the road south, stayed overnight at two way stations and reached Wakefield at dusk the third day. Marshal Winters was happy to put Bassett in the calaboose. "Where's the other one?"

"He put up a fight," Reb said gravely. "Not a really good decision on his part."

"He lost . . ."

"I'm afraid so."

5

Winters sent a note to the bank, advising them that the money had been recovered. He said to Reb, "How much of this you figger they spent?"

"Only a few dollars. I doubt if they wanted anyone in Huntling to know they had it, so they didn't go on a spree and throw it around. They'd save that for Vetter or some big town."

"Umm, I 'spect so."

Manager Dolan came to the office at once, rubbing his hands together. "You got our money?"

"It's all here," Winters said, "or almost all."

Dolan looked into the saddlebags and smiled at Reb. "How'd you get it?"

Reb recounted the chase and how he had found the two men. Winters said, "The tall one, Hinks, tried to shoot it out, and they'll bury him there. T'other one's in the jail, shot in the hand. You owe my friend here six hunnerd dollars." He glanced at Reb. "That's the posted reward."

Dolan nodded glumly. "Yes, I expect we do. Come to the bank anytime, Mr. Reb. I'll have it ready." He took the canvas bags of money and left.

Winters winked at Reb. "Them bankers hates to pay *out* anything."

The newspaper put out an extra edition concerning the holdup and its resolution, praising Reb to the skies. Marshal Winters related to a reporter the story of the shooting in Huntling, since Reb had declined, and when it came out in the columns, it was somewhat exaggerated, Reb thought. The robbers had spent a total of twenty-seven dollars, Dolan declared, "Less than we feared. So it all came out well."

Except for the one who had lost his smarts at a critical time, Hinks. The circuit judge would try the other thief, Bassett, in a week or two. The final judgment was not in doubt, the paper said. Bassett would spend years in prison.

Billy Cook was spending his days sleeping, Deputy Jim said. And when he was awake, he was yelling for this or that. He wanted coffee or tobacco, or shouted for Jim to come and play cards with him, through the bars.

Jim said he usually closed the jail door and took a chair outside, to sit where he couldn't hear the clamor.

"If you have no objections," Reb said to Marshal Winters, "I'll leave my horse here in your stable and take Billy back to Carter by stage. I have to come back for the trial. . . ."

"Hell's fire, anything you want! You're cock-o'-the-walk in this town right now, son." He looked at the calendar hanging on the wall behind his desk. "The judge ought t'be here in nine days, give'r take a few. He's usual on the dot."

Billy was happy to see the last of the jail; unhappy at going back to Carter, and whining to be manacled, it being very uncomfortable. Nothing pleased Billy for very long, and Reb did not try. He complained about the jarring bouncing of the coach, about the weather, which had turned hot, about the food and cramped accommodations at the way stations, and about how people stared at him in irons.

Reb closed his ears to all of it.

He was delighted to turn the prisoner over to the sheriff in Carter. A sitting judge with not too many cases included Billy, and found him guilty within days. Billy was shipped off to the territorial prison without delay.

Reb collected his fifty dollars, and when Billy was shown to be also a cow thief, he collected another hundred. He sent the fifty to the bank in St. Louis, along with the six hundred he'd gotten from Mr. Dolan at the bank. His account was looking much more respectable all at once. Now, if he could collect the offered fifteen hundred . . .

He had begun thinking about the future; he could not always be a bounty hunter. The law attracted him. With his savings, he might enter law school and hang out a shingle—maybe even become a judge. It was something to dream about. . . .

When Reb saw Julia, things did not go well. He met her one afternoon on the boardwalk and they chatted, sitting on a bench by a photographer's shop. She had a new ring, which she displayed proudly. She was engaged to be married to the son of a feed-store owner. He was a young man with a good, solid job in his father's emporium, which he would one day inherit. She implied that Reb had no job and little future. He had to admit she had a point.

But, of course, he did not want a job, and he did not try to explain that to her. He had lost the campaign before it had really started. And probably it was just as well.

He wished her well and took the next stagecoach back to Wakefield. According to Marshal Winter's calendar, the judge was due to arrive the next day.

He had been in Wakefield, at the hotel, only a few hours when a message came for him. The president of the town council, George Gibbons, invited him to the Red Rooster for a drink and conversation.

Reb had just come up from the bathhouse, where he'd washed off the dust and grime of the three-day trip. He was lying on the bed, enjoying the feel of a mattress instead of a leather-sprung coach seat, when the clerk brought the note.

He looked at his watch—it was late in the afternoon. What did Gibbons want?

He pulled on his boots, combed his hair, and stretched. The president of the council was an important man. His invitation was tantamount to a command. Besides, Reb was curious. He went downstairs and along the street to the fancy saloon, a hurdy-gurdy, dance-hall combination. The dance hall was open, but the band was not playing as he entered the swinging doors. The girls were drifting into the large hall; things would get noisy in a short while. About two dozen men were in the saloon, standing about in groups, talking and laughing.

A well-dressed portly man came toward him, holding out his hand. "I'm Gibbons. Thanks for coming, Mr. Wiley."

He had a soft hand. He looked about fifty, graying about the temples, obviously well fed. He had a courtly manner and a well-modulated voice. He led Reb to a table near the wall, away from the dance-hall side, and lifted a finger to a barman. "Sit down, Mr. Wiley. . . ."

"Folks call me Reb."

"As I will, then, with your permission. What will you drink, sir?"

"Beer."

Gibbons said, "I've heard about you from Bill Winters. He thinks you're something, you know. Was that story about you in the *Democrat* accurate—about your fight with the two holdup men?"

"In general, yes."

Gibbons offered him a cigar from a tooled leather case. "I know that Bill would love to have you as deputy. . . ." He sighed. "But we can't afford it. We scrape together the money for his part-time deputy, and we're all ashamed of what we pay Bill. I'm thankful we're not one of those hell-for-leather towns where the law is in danger every night. We have no real crime in Wakefield. The bank robbery was our first—except for the shootings of Mr. Chartis and the manager, Aiken. Those were not street crimes, as you know."

A bartender came to the table, wiping his hands on his apron. Gibbons said, "Beer for my friend and myself, Harry."

"You bet, Mr. Gibbons." The man hurried away.

Gibbons struck a match and held it under Reb's cigar. "The two murders are a most exasperating case. We can't discover a motive for the killings, and without that, I'm afraid we'll never find the killer. I feel the same as Bill, that he's laughing at us."

"You think as the marshal does, that it's someone still here in town?"

"Well, yes and no. I don't know what to think, really. That's why I say it's exasperating." He lit his own cigar, puffing blue smoke. "We've had session after session about it, trying to think of something. . . ." He sighed deeply. "We did find out one thing—that Chartis and Aiken knew each other in the east, before they came here. So it's possible to suppose that someone might have had it in for them—for whatever reason—and followed them here. Is that far-fetched?"

Reb shrugged. "Hard to say . . ."

"The trouble with a thing like this is that we cannot ask the principal players in the piece. They're both dead."

The bartender brought the beer and departed. Reb asked, "Why did you invite me here, Mr. Gibbons?"

The portly man smiled. "So you can earn fifteen hundred dollars. That's the amount of the reward."

Reb sipped the beer. "This case is called a mystery by all of you. It's a case for someone with police training."

"Perhaps, but there's no one closer than a thousand miles who has that requirement. Bill tells me you have brains and imagination. The reward is substantial. I hope you'll give it a try."

Reb took a long breath and gazed over the room. He had the money to support himself for a long while without income—and Gibbons was right, the reward *was* substantial. Could he unravel the "mystery"? Or would he spend a month and gain nothing? The killer might be hundreds of miles away in a safe hideout.

But he would never know unless . . .

He said to Gibbons, "Let me talk again to Marshal Winters. Then I'll decide."

The other nodded. "Good enough."

6

In the marshal's office Reb sat by the desk as Winters put his feet up on an open drawer and puffed his cigar. The older man regarded his visitor mildly, blue eyes peering out from under the hat brim. "You going to look into this here case, Reb?"

"Tell me about Chartis and the other one—what's his name?"

"Joe Aiken. About all I know concernin' Homer Chartis is he owned the largest store in the territory and was cheap as a politician's promise. He was tight, too. He squeezed ever' dollar, and everybody worked for him hated him. That's what they told me."

"He was married. . . ."

"Yeah. And they say he was jealous of her. A sweet woman, far's anybody knows. He didn't deserve her."

"You've met her?"

"Once'r twice. Seemed a fluttery female and totally helpless." Winters shrugged. "Think she was quite a bit younger'n Homer."

"You say everybody hated him?"

"Well, none of his employees come to the funeral. They all did for Joe Aiken."

"And Homer's wife?"

"She was there, wearing a veil so's we never seen her face. Seemed to take it hard. Homer's death, I mean."

"Did you learn if Chartis bawled out any of the employees—or fired anybody—anything of the sort?"

"I asked around, but they was a bunch of clams. Nobody wanted to tell me nothing."

"How many employees?"

Winters frowned. "Five, I think. Yeah, five counting the bookkeeper. They all still there."

"Is Mrs. Chartis running the business now?"

"No. She got a manager right off, John Franken. I doubt if she been in the store. She wouldn't know the first thing about it. Franken was a clerk. I guess he'd been there the longest."

Reb nodded, noting down the names. "What about Joe Aiken?"

"He was a widower. His wife died years ago, before he come to Wakefield. He was a good-looking man—a lot of the church ladies set their caps for him, they tell me. He was big in the Methodist Church—sang in the choir, you know."

"Was he considered a good manager?"

"The others say so."

"Did he get along with Chartis?"

Winters made a face. "That's a hard question. I doubt if anybody did. But Aiken was manager for a long time, so I guess he did."

"But you have doubts about whether they were killed because of the robbery?"

"Well, yeah . . ."

"Maybe they fought back?"

"There was no evidence of that." Winters took off his hat and looked at it, brushed off some dust and laid it aside. "I figger they might both have been involved in something, maybe from years ago, and it caught up with them."

"Revenge?"

"That's a powerful thing, revenge. Maybe."

Reb rocked his chair back and forth, frowning at the street. "I hope it's not revenge. And not from a long time ago. Because if it is, chances are the killer is long gone. He wouldn't hang around after he did what he came here for. At least I doubt if he would."

Winters nodded. "That listens good. You probably right." He puffed clouds of smoke. "But what else?"

Reb smiled. "There're lots of sins. Right now, pick one."

"I'm an old man. I don't sin no more. You pick one."

John Franken did not seem particularly glad to see him, Reb thought. He tried to hide it with a painted-on smile, offering Reb a chair in his cluttered office. "I understand you're working with Marshal Winters . . . ?"

"Yes, I am." Franken had been Joseph Aiken's assistant manager for several years and knew all the details of the store. He was a slow-moving, horse-faced man with closely cropped brown hair. He wore rimless specs perched on a thick nose, and he bent his head to look over them at Reb. He seemed a dry-as-dust man, in a brown untailored suit and tie with brown shoes.

And probably had brown opinions, Reb thought, seating himself.

Franken began by expressing his regrets that Mr. Chartis and Joe Aiken were gone. He trusted that Reb would be able to uncover the truth and bring the culprit to justice.

Reb promised he would do his best. "Why do you think the two were killed, Mr. Franken?"

"I have no idea, sir. I believe the marshal was quoted as saying it might have been robbery."

"No large sum was taken. . . ."

"But what other reason could there have been?"

Did the man have no imagination? Reb shrugged off the question. "How long have you worked for Mr. Chartis?"

"Since Mr. Chartis went into business—fifteen years ago. He and his father had a store in Vetter. Mr. Chartis sold out when his father died. He got married soon after and came here to Wakefield—and bought this building from me."

"From you?"

Franken smiled at his visitor's surprise. "Yes, my grandfather built it and rented it to several tenants. My father was never interested in a retail business, so I inherited it. I was glad to sell it to Homer because I had no capital to go into business with. So I went to work for him and learned the business from the ground up.'' He made a vague gesture. ''I had hoped to become manager, but Joe Aiken had much more experience. . . .''

''And you became Aiken's assistant.''

''Yes. And I hurry to add, very good friends also.''

''Are you married, Mr. Franken?''

''No. I'm not—no more.''

''How close were you to Homer Chartis?''

''Not very. No one was. Joe and I often walked home together—we lived close by. And often we stopped for a beer and discussed the problems of the store.''

''Did he have problems with Chartis?''

''Well, yes, he did. Mostly I suppose because he was the manager and his ideas were frequently opposed by Homer.'' Franken sighed. ''Homer did not like change. He liked things to stay the same, and Joe Aiken wanted to move forward.''

''In what way?''

''In sales mostly. He wanted to sell more goods—to find out what the customers wanted to buy. But Mr. Chartis didn't seem to care. Joe told me often that Chartis was satisfied with the store as it was.''

''So they quarreled?''

''I suppose so. I never heard them, but Joe said they had arguments.''

''I'm told that Mr. Chartis was generally disliked.''

''I'm afraid that's true.''

Reb paused. ''Enough so that one of the employees might have shot him?''

Franken made a helpless little gesture. ''I don't know. I doubt it. But then, why shoot Joe Aiken? He wasn't disliked.''

''Do you know whether Aiken and Chartis knew each other before they came west?''

''No, I don't.''

* * *

Reb wrote out a message to Mrs. Chartis, asking to speak to her. Three days went by before he received an answer. Then she asked in a note what he wanted.

He sent a reply, stating that he was investigating her husband's murder. Marshal Winters appended a note saying Reb was working with him. She replied that she was in no state at present to discuss the matter.

"I tol' you, she's a fluttery female," Winters said. "It might take her a month to settle down. The murder musta been a helluva shock to her." He puffed his cigar. "I dunno what she can tell you anyways. She never told me nothing." He eyed Reb. "You turn up anything yet?"

"No, not really. But one thing bothers me."

"What?"

"Aiken's murder. Why did the killer shoot him? I can understand someone getting even with Chartis—he was the big boss—but why Aiken?"

Winters took off his hat and looked at the crease. "I been wonderin' that ever since it happened. They ain't any good answer."

"There must be an answer!"

"Umm." Winters put the hat on again. "What if Aiken saw the feller who shot Mr. Chartis? That would give the feller a reason to shoot Aiken."

"Then why didn't Aiken come to you at once?"

Winters pried himself out of the chair. "Let's go have some lunch."

The robber, Bob Bassett, was a growling, snarling prisoner, swearing at anyone who came near the bars. He even swore at the doctor who came in once a week to look at the hand. The wound was gradually healing, but it pained him constantly and made his nights more than uncomfortable.

The circuit judge came to town on a Monday and took most of the day getting himself settled. He was not the same judge who'd been riding the circuit for years. And he was two weeks late. On Tuesday and Wednesday he handled small matters that had been hanging fire, and scheduled Bassett's trial for Thursday.

Bassett was brought from the jail by Marshal Winters and seated in the courtroom while a jury was selected. A local lawyer had been named to defend him; he saw his client for the first time and they sat with heads together as the lawyer made notes.

The jurymen decided upon, the judge rapped with his gavel and asked Bassett how he pleaded.

"Not guilty," Bassett said, and half a dozen in the courtroom laughed.

The judge was a sallow-faced man in his fifties, named Tasker. He had a large head and great shocks of dark hair. His spectacles slid down his nose as he frowned at the audience. "That's enough o' that." He pointed at the prosecutor.

"Your Honor," the prosecutor said, "the accused was caught in possession of the money belonging to the Wakefield Bank. Their wrappers were still around the bills. Two witnesses will attest that he was one of the two men who abducted them and forced them to open the bank's safe. The second robber is now dead."

Tasker looked at the defending lawyer, who said, "Nothing at this time, Your Honor."

"Then let's hear the witnesses."

"I call Mr. Feeny," the prosecutor said.

Timothy Feeny was pale and sunken-cheeked. His clothes hung on him, and he used a cane as he walked to the witness chair. The clerk swore him in, and he sat down and stared at the prisoner.

The prosecutor asked him several questions, his occupation and whether or not he recalled the events of the night the bank was robbed. Then he asked if one of the two robbers was in the courtroom.

Feeny pointed to Bassett. "That's him. He's the short one."

"You're positive?"

''Absolutely positive. He threatened to kill me and my wife if we didn't open the safe.''

Bassett's lawyer stood up, then sat down again, shaking his head. Bassett glared at him.

Mrs. Feeny was called and she also identified Bassett.

Then Reb was called to the witness chair. He told how he had followed the two men and found them in Huntling. He was sorry, he said, that he'd been forced to shoot Dave Hinks, but he'd had no choice. He'd shot Bassett through the hand and found the bank's money in their saddlebags.

Bassett could not deny his wound. The judge found him guilty and sentenced him to ten years in the territorial prison, at hard labor.

As Marshal Winters was leading him out, Bassett yelled that he'd be back to kill Feeny.

Winters backhanded him and pushed him through the door.

7

Reb listened carefully to everything that was said at the trial, but it was an open-and-shut case. Bassett had no defense; the prosecutor and judge merely went through the motions; the defense attorney was impotent to affect the outcome, and Bassett went to prison.

Nevertheless it was interesting—the workings of the law—and Reb determined to sit in on more trials . . . when he had the opportunity.

He talked to the other store employees, beginning with the accountant, Tyler Cole. Cole was a stringy, middle-aged man with thick spectacles and white hair. He looked much older than he was, and apparently paid little attention to dress. His clothes were badly wrinkled, even shabby, and his office reflected that trait. It was cluttered and untidy, shelves jammed with folders and papers, with wastebaskets full of crumpled paper.

He had no opinion, or so he said, of the shootings. He said, "I don't know anything about them or why the two men were shot. I'm told that Mrs. Chartis is going to continue with the store, and that's good enough for me."

"You don't seem to care one way or the other."

"Oh, I care about the job." Cole shrugged thin shoulders. "I like this job. I pay the others and myself every week, and go over the accounts with the manager—whoever he is—pay the bills and do what I'm told. That's it."

"Were you friendly with Mr. Chartis?"

"Nobody was, that I know of. I do my job and don't worry about that."

"Do you wonder why they were killed?"

Cole gave him the ghost of a smile. "It crossed my mind—to wonder, but that's as far as it got. Do *you* know why they were killed?"

"No, I don't. Are you married, Mr. Cole?"

"I am not. I'm fifty-three now. I was married, a long time ago, but we separated. Women are a chore. Take up too much of your time."

Reb smiled. "Thank you, Mr. Cole." He left the office, shaking his head. Cole was an old woman himself and didn't know it.

Axel Lynch and Jody Fogle were clerks in the store. They were both younger men, trying to make ends meet on the meager salaries they were paid. Both men complained of this within moments as Reb questioned them. They worked long hours, Lynch said, and were expected to stay late, after the store closed, to rearrange merchandise and sweep the floors. They got one day a week off, Sunday, and never a kind word from Chartis.

They had both liked Joe Aiken better. When things were slack or when Chartis was away from the store, he allowed them to rest off their feet, or go out into the alley for a smoke. They both agreed that since Chartis was gone, their lives were easier. The new manager, John Franken, was one of them and knew their problems; he had been chief clerk only recently.

Mrs. Chartis, they said, never came into the store at all since her husband had passed into the beyond. Before that she had appeared once or twice a week for short visits.

Neither man had any idea why Chartis and Aiken had been killed or had any guesses about who had done the crimes.

And neither had the deliveryman, Seth Buckley, or the storeroom clerk, Ben Kepler. Buckley was only nineteen and was in the store only a few hours a day, and always at the back of the store, where he readied boxes and packages for shipment and piled them in his buckboard. He owned his own mare and wagon and also worked for another store in town. Ben Kepler was a nervous sort who protested that he knew nothing at all about the murders and was very uncooperative, saying he wanted to be left alone.

Reb said to Marshal Winters in the jail office, "None of them knows anything—or so they say."

Both shootings had taken place at night, long after the day's business, when all the employees had gone home and the store was locked. The next day, when Aiken's body was discovered, the lantern in his office was still lighted, and so was one in the storeroom. There was apparently no connection.

Winters said, "Mr. Chartis must have let the killer in—or he had a key. Same for Aiken. Franken told me that Aiken had suggested to Chartis that the store locks be changed, as an ordinary precaution, since it hadn't been done in years. But Chartis was cheap, a penny-pincher, and refused."

"Could someone have hidden himself in the store during the day?"

"I thought of that, but the clerks say it's not possible."

Reb shook his head. "Maybe they said so, but I think it's possible. I looked around. It's a big store with lots of nooks and crannies."

"Ummm. But how would the killer know Mr. Chartis would be there after hours?"

"Good point," Reb agreed. "Maybe he had knowledge of Chartis's habits. And of course, too, maybe he was meeting Chartis there after hours when they wouldn't be disturbed."

"There was no note on the body or on the desk. . . ."

"The killer would be sure to have taken it if there had been. The offices were both ransacked."

"Yes." Winters rolled a cigar in his thick fingers and sniffed it. "It sure looks to me like it was somebody from outside. Somebody we don't know."

"I hope you're not right, because if you are, he's sitting by a fire in Kansas City warming his toes this very minute."

"Well, we settled that." The marshal smiled. "Now, tell me, why'd he do it?"

Reb sent another carefully worded note to Mrs. Chartis, asking for an interview, and she replied that she would see him in a week.

In the meantime he went to the store and studied both offices, more for something to do than anything else. Marshal Winters went with him. Chartis's office was large and comfortable-looking. It had been cleaned up and swept out. It had a solid teak desk and upholstered chairs, landscapes on the walls, and a thick turkey carpet.

Winters pointed to the chair by the desk. "He was shot right there, in that chair, while he was sittin' at the desk. It got blood every damn where. It musta took them a week to sop it all up."

"So someone came into the room behind him?"

"Or was already there. The office door was open when we found 'im. No tellin' if it was that night. He woulda heard it open. Of course, somebody might have said something, too, someone he knew was there or expected."

Reb nodded in agreement. Probably Chartis had known the mystery killer. Of course, if the door had been open, a stranger might have sneaked in and shot him. He glanced at the stout marshal. "How could a stranger get into the store?"

"He stole a key."

"Nobody reported one missing."

"You said he hid in one of the nooks and crannies in the daytime."

"Yes, he might have. So we agree on premeditated murder for both?"

The marshal took off his hat and slapped it against his leg. "Yes. Neither one of them shot theirselves."

"Did Chartis have any other employee that he discharged for one reason or another in the past?"

"Yes, I think he did, but let's ask Franken. He'll know for sure."

John Franken had taken over Joe Aiken's office and made it his own. Everything was rearranged, even the placement of the main desk. He had taken down the pictures and put up different ones, mostly military scenes of the cavalry.

At Reb's question he said, "Yes, two employees, clerks, were let go because they were no good. One a long time ago, maybe ten years. The other, only two or three years ago. I remember when it happened."

"What can you tell us about them?"

"Let's see if there's anything in the files. . . ." Franken opened a cabinet and searched in a low drawer for a few minutes, bringing out several folders. "The recent one was Diego Ranny. He was nineteen when he was let go. Unmarried, living in a boardinghouse."

"What was the reason?"

Franken smiled. "He told Aiken he could read, and he couldn't. So he was no good as a clerk, he made too many mistakes." He pulled a printed square of newsprint from the folder. "But you won't pin anything on him. Look at this."

Reb frowned. It was a news item concerning the death by shooting of Diego Ranny in a saloon.

"Purty definite," Marshal Winters said. "What about the other one?"

"There's nothing in the files about him. I suppose because it was so long ago. If Aiken kept old files, they'll be in the storeroom. I'd have to plow through some boxes. . . ."

"We'd take it kindly," Winters said.

"All right. Give me a few days."

8

John Franken came by the jail office after store hours to notify Marshal Winters that one of the store employees, Ben Kepler, had not reported for work for three days.

Winters was annoyed. "Not for three goddamn days! How come you took your time before tellin' me?"

"I thought he might be sick."

"Is he?"

"No—at least not in his room. He rents a room from Mrs. Wilson. I sent a boy over there, and she said he hasn't been home for days. Three days."

Winters waved him out. "I'll look into it."

He talked to Reb in the early evening, and in the morning Reb rode to the boardinghouse. It was owned and run by a widow, Mrs. Leon Wilson. She was a big buxom woman in a blue dress and frilly apron. She frowned at Reb, head back, studying him through steel-rimmed glasses.

"I dunno where Ben got to. He ain't been in for supper for three days, and his bed ain't been slept in."

"Have you any idea where he might have gone?"

She pursed her lips. "He got a sister in Eagleton—that's in Missouri. But he wouldn't have took off for there without tellin' me. Besides, his clothes and fixin's is still in his room. Horse's gone, though."

"Then you didn't see him saddle up and leave?"

"No." Her voice turned hard. "I woulda asked him where he's going, wouldn't I?"

"Yes, of course you would." Reb smiled winningly. "Can you tell me something about his habits, Mrs. Wilson?"

"Well, he come home here from the store every night—hardly ever missed supper. He been with me for near six year. Then he'd go back to the Hole Card—that's a saloon—and talk for a few hours. That's his only pleasure. He's a quiet man. Never had no ruckus with nobody."

"Was he particular friends with anyone?"

She shook her head. "Not particular, no. But he's a friendly man, Ben is. Everybody likes him."

They had talked about Ben's disappearance around the supper table, Mrs. Wilson said. No one who lived in the house had any idea what had happened to him. But they were all curious why he had taken his horse. He customarily walked to and from the store.

The Hole Card Saloon was a small room, compared to some. It was owned by a short, black-haired man named Corvus Legg, who resembled a pirate. Reb lounged at the bar, sipping a beer, and asked him about Ben Kepler.

"Ben works at the big gen'ral store."

"And he comes here evenings."

"Yeah, been doing it for years."

"But you haven't seen him lately."

Legg made a face. "No, not for a couple days. Why you askin' about him?"

"Because no one knows where he is. If he didn't come here, where would he be likely to go?"

Legg turned down his lips. "How the hell would I know that?"

"All right." Reb glanced at the quiet room. "Point out a couple of his close friends."

In a snarling voice. "You a lawman?"

Reb fixed the other with a steely eye. "So far I've been polite."

Legg took a long breath, studying the bulk of the man across the bar. He looked at the red headband and at Reb's wrists, and evidently thought better of what he might have said. ‘‘Over there, that end table. Them two, Bud and Lennie. You ast them.’’

Reb smiled. ‘‘Thanks.’’

He moved across the room, pulled out a chair and sat opposite the two surprised men. ‘‘Mind if I sit down, gents?’’

The heavier of the two said, ‘‘Who’re you?’’

‘‘Mr. Legg tells me you’re Bud and Lennie. Which is which?’’

The heavy man said, ‘‘I’m Bud.’’ He was grizzled, with a ruddy face and short reddish hair. He wore a dark blue wool cap pulled down to his ears, a yellow-checked shirt buttoned to the neck, and there was a pipe on the table in front of him.

Lennie was half his companion’s size, pale-faced and slightly better dressed, with small hands holding a deck of cards. He said, ‘‘What you want wi’ us?’’

‘‘My name is Reb Wiley and I’m interested in finding out what happened to your friend Ben Kepler.’’

‘‘Ahhhhh, Ben,’’ Bud said. ‘‘Yeah, we been wondering that, too. We ain’t seen ’im for a couple days.’’

‘‘Why you want t’know about him?’’ Lennie asked.

Reb said, ‘‘I’m looking into the murder of Mr. Chartis and his manager, Mr. Aiken. I want to ask Ben some questions. He may know something important.’’

‘‘You don’t think he killed Chartis?’’ Bud scowled. ‘‘Ben wouldn’t hurt nobody.’’

‘‘I’m positive he did not, but he worked at the store. I have to talk to every one of them. You both saw him daily. What can you tell me about him?’’

They both looked at each other. It was obvious they had never contemplated such a question.

Reb said, ‘‘Did he speak to either of you recently about going anywhere? Mrs. Wilson at the boardinghouse mentioned his sister in Missouri. . . .’’

Bud scratched his jaw and picked up the pipe. ‘‘He never said anything about going there.’’ He glanced at Lennie, who shook his head.

‘‘He never mentioned going anywhere.’’

"Mrs. Wilson thinks he may have gone suddenly. He took nothing from his room, but his horse is gone from the stable. Did he have any enemies?"

Lennie looked surprised. "Enemies? Ben Kepler? Hell no."

"Can either of you think of a place Ben might have gone if he was in a hurry—maybe thought someone might be after him?"

"Naw," Bud said. "Nobody'd be after Ben." He took out a knife and scratched inside the bole of the pipe.

"Wait a minute," Lennie said softly. "What if he went to the cabin?"

"What cabin?"

"Ummm, yeah, he might have," Bud agreed.

"What cabin?"

Lennie said, "It's mostly a shack. Us and a few others built it years ago. We useta go deer hunting up there in the hills, but we haven't used it in a spell."

"Maybe five years," Bud put in. "Yeah, he might have gone there . . . but why would he want to?"

"I'm guessing," Reb said. "Maybe to stay alive."

"Stay alive?" Bud scowled.

"Maybe he knows something—about the murders. If he went to the cabin, he has a reason. Can you tell me where it is?"

Lennie got up and went to the bar. He came back with a square of paper and a stub of pencil. With Bud looking over his shoulder with advice, he laboriously drew a map. The two argued over distances and landmarks, but agreed finally on a compromise. The cabin was at the edge of the woods, well under the trees, in a valley and several hundred yards from a creek. It was a shallow valley with gentle slopes, and heavily wooded. The cabin could be found by means of a sharp bend in the stream and a pile of black rocks higher than a man's head.

"They got Indian writin' on them," Bud said. "There's other black rocks around, but these is in a pile, hard to miss."

Lennie added, ''The cabin is just north of the rocks, in the trees. You got to hunt for it—if you're going there.''

''No choice,'' Reb said. ''I want to find him.''

9

Reb went from the Hole Card to the jail office and talked to Marshal Winters, telling him what he'd learned from Bud and Lennie. The other studied the crude map. "How far they say this cabin is?"

"About twenty miles northwest of here. That would put it just about north of Fort Hayes."

Winters nodded. "That's mighty up-and-down country, some of it." He squinted at Reb. "You figger this Ben knows something?"

"I don't know what to think. But I'm curious as hell. Why did he take off in such a hurry? Of course, it might have nothing at all to do with the murders. He took nothing much with him, so far as I can discover. If he went to the cabin, it might have been a first thought, but unless it's stocked with food, it's not going to be a place to hide out for very long."

"Could be canned provisions there."

"Maybe. Bud and Lennie say it hasn't been used for five years. How long does a can of food last?"

"Damn if I know. I guess if you set an airtight in the sun, it might last for a day'r two." Winters took off his hat, looked inside it, and put it back on. "So if he gets hungry, he won't be there when you show up."

"But I've got to go. If he's running from someone—it might be the someone we want. D'you have a rifle I can borrow?"

"Help yourself." The marshal pointed to the rack. "You want Jim to go along with you?"

"I'd rather go alone." Reb selected a .44 Winchester and made sure it was loaded.

"When you going?"

"Right away." Reb went to the door. "See you in a couple days."

He bought food and a box of shells; they would fit both the rifle and his .44 pistol. He saddled the bay and rode out about noon, taking the Elland road west. Why had Ben skedaddled—in such a hurry? What did he know? Reb had not gained the impression, when he'd talked to Ben in the storeroom, that the other was a deep thinker. Could he have panicked and run? It certainly seemed like it. It was possible he had guilty knowledge—and the killer knew it or found out about it. Did anything else make sense?

Reb had been this way before, when he'd gone after the bank robbers, Hinks and Bassett. Then, he'd skirted the hills and headed into the desert after crossing the north and south Vetter road. Now, he made for the hills, looking for tracks, but found none of a single horseman. It was a wide land; if Ben had come this way, he might easily have taken another route.

When Reb reached them, the hills were a jumble, as if some giant hand had crumpled and dropped them and left them to gather brush and trees. Bud and Lennie had mentioned a stream; it flowed eventually into the Hayes River, and he looked for it, making slow progress along the slopes. He had to pick his way, and dusk came inevitably, forcing him to halt and make camp.

He dug a pit for a fire, heated meat and coffee, then covered the fire and moved a mile or more from the spot to settle down for the night. He had heard Indian scouts talk of this precaution. It had saved their bacon, they said, a number of times.

In the morning he came on the stream near midday and followed it north, keeping an eye out for the black rocks. The stream flowed noisily through a shallow valley, splashing over a rocky bed as it hurried south, snaking through a green meadow several hundred yards wide. Reb stayed in the shelter of the trees, walking the bay.

He barely heard the distant shot—but felt it rap into the horse. The bay took several halting steps, stumbled, and went down heavily. Grabbing the Winchester from the boot, Reb rolled free. He was in a shallow fold of ground fringed by tall weeds. Three more shots came in quick succession, seeking him, cutting the dirt inches over his head. He had no chance to look for the sniper as he pressed himself into the earth. Someone was a damned good shot! Probably had a rifle with a scope.

He inched forward along the ground, trying not to disturb the weeds, but another shot came so close, he could almost taste its passing. The sniper was across the stream in the woods somewhere.

Had he been followed from town?

He looked back at the bay horse. The animal was very dead. Reb swore aloud. The sniper had put him afoot, miles from any habitation. This was the last thing he'd expected. It could not be Ben Kepler firing at him, could it, thinking he was an enemy? Was Ben a marksman? No one had mentioned it. Maybe the someone who was after Ben had put him afoot.

Ahead, maybe a dozen yards, was a gully, and he slithered into it, drawing no shots. This was better; peering through the weeds, he examined the woods beyond the stream. He could detect no movement. Maybe the sniper had faded away. He looked at the sky; it was many hours till dark. The gully wound away toward the south and became deeper.

Maybe he could work his way around behind the sniper. The other would not know whether or not he had hit his target. He might think so and come to look.

But he did not. Reb waited, the Winchester ready, for an hour or so, but no one appeared. The sniper might be satisfied that he was afoot and think to finish the job later. A man traveling slowly on foot might be an easy one to ambush.

He moved south along the gully for half a mile and paused, examining the woods again. Birds flitted among the trees, apparently not disturbed. Ahead of him was a gentle grassy slope to the creek, which seemed very shallow. On the far side the trees came closer, but if he crossed, he would be in the open for a good hundred yards—too good an opportunity for the sniper, who had proved he was an excellent shot. Did he want to try it?

He levered a shell into the chamber of the rifle. If he were fired on, he'd fire back at the smoke and keep firing, making it hot for the sniper.

Unless the other killed him with the first shot.

He selected a place to climb the bank, took a long breath, settling the .44 on his hip, inched his way to the top—and saw the horseman! The rider was moving away from him in the trees, a very long rifle shot distant. Reb scrambled to the rim of the gully and fired at the horse. Then he dashed across the stream and into the trees. But the horseman had disappeared. He found tracks that led eastward. The rider was spurring the horse. . . .

In high disgust he went back to the downed horse and pulled off the saddle and food sack. He tied them both high above ground on tree limbs, then went to look for the cabin.

The black rocks were only a mile farther on, and the cabin was where Bud and Lennie had said it would be. Behind it was a small pole corral—with Ben Kepler's horse dead inside it. Shot to death. The brown saddle was still on the body, with Ben's initials burned into it.

There was no sign of Ben Kepler.

The sniper had shot the horse but evidently missed Ben. Reb frowned at the dead animal. Why hadn't the sniper killed Ben, too? Had Ben evaded him? It was very possible that Ben had brought along a weapon and had kept the sniper at bay.

But Reb could find no fresh bullet holes in the cabin, as there might be if shots had been exchanged.

He looked for tracks. Ben had left the cabin behind—but where had he gone? Reb spent an hour searching and turned up nothing. He was not an expert man-tracker. Few were. He might track a horse, but that was quite a different matter.

A horse weighed much more than a man and had four hooves to leave tracks.

He made a wide circle about the cabin and found no trail. It was likely that Ben would head back for the town, he thought. If he had no food, or little food, it was important to find some before his strength began to fail.

Of course, he might head for Fort Hayes, it being closer than Wakefield.

Reb went back to the tree and carried the saddle and food sack to the shack. He spent the night there—without incident—and in the morning left the saddle in the cabin and began the long walk back to town.

Someone had very definitely tried to kill him, and might try again, now that he was at a disadvantage. Coming north to the cabin, he had followed the easy route, by the stream. It was foolish to go back the same way. He crossed the stream and headed up the slope to the ridge. He followed it slowly, stopping frequently to look and listen. He thought he spotted a horseman far off—but could not be positive. It might have been a deer and a trick of light.

He made a cold camp that night—and the next. He ate beans and peaches from cans and saw no one. Near midnight of the fourth day, he reached Wakefield.

Ben Kepler had not returned.

10

That night Reb spent several hours in a copper tub, soaking. His feet were sore, encased in boots for miles of rough terrain, boots not made for walking. He had limped into town, swearing with every step at the sniper who had put him afoot.

The hotel night clerk hunted up some Dr. Pearl's Foot Balm, which he rubbed on thickly before falling into bed. In the morning his feet were still swollen, and he could not get his boots on. He sent a note to the marshal, and the lawman came to the hotel and laid his hat on the bed. He listened to Reb's recounting of the shooting and subsequent happenings.

"How far you figger you walked?"

"Forty miles, give or take a dozen."

Winters chuckled. "You never seen the man who shot at you?"

"No. He kept me pinned down, and when I got into the gully, he was gone. I never caught up with him."

"You think maybe he follered you from town?"

Reb shrugged. "He might have. I don't know. I certainly didn't expect a tail, so I didn't watch my backtrail. If that's so, it means the sniper knows I'm working with you on this case."

"You ain't kept it a secret."

"No way to do that."

"Ben's horse was shot, too, huh? How long ago, when you found 'im?"

"A few days, I suppose. Probably the day Ben arrived at

the shack. I think he made sure Ben didn't go anywhere in a hurry."

The marshal nodded.

"The sniper fired at me from a distance, a long shot for a rifle. Maybe the same for Ben. He aimed at the larger target, the horse, and figured to hit the man later. How d'you like that theory?"

"I got nothin' against it." Winters puffed his cigar. "So maybe Ben's lyin' out there in the weeds some'eres, dead as a rock?"

"He might be."

"Ummm. What'd he want to kill Ben for?"

"That's an interesting question."

Winters put his hat on. "If Ben knew something about them murders, why didn't he come to me?"

"Maybe scared to. It's hard to figure what a man might think if he's under pressure."

"Ain't that a fact." The marshal looked critically at the cigar. He scratched his thinning hair. Then he got up. "You want me t'send the doc to see them feet?"

"No. They'll be fine tomorrow. Thanks anyway."

He was able to put the boots on again in the morning and walk about the room gingerly. He ought to go back to the shack for his saddle—and maybe look around for Ben's body.

He had breakfast and went to the jail office, still limping slightly. Winters was busy writing a report; the part-time deputy, Jim, was nowhere about. Reb lowered himself into a chair facing the desk. "I need a horse."

"Jed Urshel, down at the livery, got several. Where you going?"

"Thought I'd go back to the shack for my saddle."

Winters leaned on his elbows. "Whyn't you let Jim go after that saddle? You go to Fort Hayes and see if Ben went there."

"All right . . ." He was surprised when Winters jumped up, smiling, looking at the door. He glanced around as a young woman came into the office. He got up quickly.

Winters said, "This's my beautiful daughter, Lorrie. Honey, this here's Reb Wiley, I tol' you about."

She said, "Hello, Mr. Wiley."

"Nice to meet you, Miss Winters." The marshal was right, she was a beauty. She had light brown hair pulled back and tied with a yellow ribbon at the nape of her neck. She wore no hat. Her cheekbones were rounded and her skin pale; she looked no more than twenty. Her dress was blue and had white lace and a hint of bustle. She was folding a blue parasol as she came in.

She said, "You forgot to give me the kitchen money this morning, Daddy. . . ."

"Oh—Oh yes." Winters patted his pockets and drew an envelope from inside his coat, handing it over. "Sorry."

She took it with a smile and went to the door. "It was nice to meet you, Mr. Wiley." She went out, and Reb started breathing again. What a vision!

He wanted to go to the door and watch her walk away, but sat down instead.

The marshal said, "Ain't she a knockout? Looks like her mother did at that age." He took a long breath and flopped in the desk chair again.

Reb said, "I never asked you—about your wife."

"She's gone, five'r six year ago. Pneumonia, the doc said. Lorrie and I keeps house now. She was away two years to one of them finishing schools. . . ."

"Like a college."

"Yeah, I guess so." The marshal took off his hat. "Now she's back, I'm scared to death she'll marry somebody and move away." He sighed deeply and put the hat on again. "I get to feelin' sorry for m'self. What was we saying?"

"You said Jim would go for my saddle and I go to Fort Hayes."

"Ain't that a good idea?"

"Probably. I'm curious as hell about Ben Kepler."

"And why he didn't come to see me. I wonder if some of the others in the store knows anything."

Reb shrugged. "If so, they've had plenty of chances to tell us."

He went down the street to the livery stable and talked to the owner, Jed Urshel. Jed was a man about sixty, white hair down over his ears, and a squint. He wore red john L's with no shirt and tattered jeans. Sure he had a horse.

"You wanna buy one or you want 'im by the day?"

"By the day, and a saddle with a rifle boot."

Jed nodded. "Come on out back to the corral."

He had five horses, and Reb picked a sorrel. He signed a paper and rode to see the local undertaker, Bartlet. The building was on a side street, framed with a false front. The two small windows had been painted black on the inside; the front door was black, with a small sign: ENTER. Across the front of the building was a large sign: UNDERTAKING PARLOUR *Dr. Jms Bartlet, Prop. Also Palms Read.*

Reb tied the horse to a hitch pole and went inside. A bell tinkled. He was in a wide room with a dozen or more newly finished coffins stacked against two walls. In a moment a man clad in black frock coat and shiny cravat came from a back room and smiled at him. "I'm Dr. Bartlet."

"Good morning, Doctor. Palms read?"

Bartlet showed him white teeth. "My wife does that, yes. Did you want a reading, sir?"

"No. I'm working with Marshal Winters. You buried Homer Chartis and Joseph Aiken. . . ."

Bartlet looked surprised. "Yes, I did." His brows went up, furrowing his smooth forehead.

"What can you tell me about the murders, Doctor?"

"I've already told the marshal all I know—there isn't much to tell, sir."

"Please tell me."

"They were both shot, either with the same gun or the same caliber. Each shot was identical, to the back of the head at very close range, maybe a foot or two. Only one shot to each. No more was needed."

"You have probably seen hundreds of gunshot wounds."

"Oh yes."

"Was there anything out of the ordinary about these?"

Bartlet shook his head slowly. "I don't think so . . . except one thing. The shooter was an expert, and he fired through a cushion in each case, to help deaden the sound, I reckon." He made a face, drawing down his thin lips. "Though I doubt if the shots could be heard in the street without that precaution."

"Nothing else?"

The man in black shook his head sadly. "No, nothing but the mystery. Apparently no one knows who did the shootings." He clasped his hands together in a dejected pose. "It's too bad. I wish there was more I could do to help. It's a terrible thing."

"Yes it is," Reb said to himself as he left the rather seedy parlor. There was a dull clatter of hooves on the street, and he waited while a wagon rumbled by. He was no closer to a solution than the day he'd started.

He left Wakefield the next morning, early. A few rags of clouds were out, with a cold breeze from the west as he took the Elland road to the cutoff. A sturdy sign, hammered into weeds, informed him that Fort Hayes was five miles distant. He crossed a swift hill stream where tiny pink flowers gathered in swatches on the banks, and reached the post in the middle of the afternoon, a drab and dreary group of buildings set down around a wide parade ground with a flagpole in the center.

It was a smaller military post than he'd expected. It was surrounded by flat, brown fields, and there was a curved sign over the road: FORT HAYES. Beside the sign was a sentry box. Two troopers rose from a bench and inquired about his business. He replied that he'd come for information about a missing citizen, and was directed to the commanding officer's building. "They's a small flag out front, and you'll see the sign over the door."

"Thanks."

He got down and wrapped the reins about a hitch rack,

and a thick-set sergeant came out onto the porch and greeted him. "A single civilian?" he said to Reb's question. "Yes, we had one in here a few days ago. Came in on foot. Why don't you go talk to Sergeant Zeller over at the stable. I think the gent bought him a horse." He pointed out the stable.

Sergeant Zeller was a thin, dark man with a drooping mustache. He admitted to selling a horse to a civilian. "Hosses is the thing we got most of."

Zeller had thrown in an old McClellan saddle, and said the buyer had told him he'd been in the cavalry in the war.

Most of the men on the post had joined up since that fracus, Zeller went on, but they had a few veterans, older men who were coming close to pension time. Being a veteran, the newcomer was asked to stay for evening mess, and he gladly accepted.

"And he met an old buddy," Zeller said. "Sergeant Schneider and him rode together with Bedford Forrest! Ain't that something, after all them years! The two of them talked most of the night."

Reb said, "I'd like to talk to Sergeant Schneider. . . ."

Zeller sent a man to Schneider's quarters after Retreat, and the sergeant showed up at the stable. "Who's looking for me?"

Reb introduced himself. "Sergeant Zeller tells me you met Ben Kepler here a few days ago."

"Yeah, I did." Schneider was a whipcord-lean man with a weathered face, smooth-shaven. "You a friend of his?"

"I've only met him once. I'm hoping he can help us with an investigation. He may know something—and not realize he knows it."

"What kind of investigation?"

"Two men were murdered in Wakefield. You may have read about it, Chartis and Aiken. Ben worked for Chartis in the store."

"Yes, I read about it. You after Ben, are you?"

Reb shook his head. "We have no evidence against Ben.

I'm hoping to get lucky. As I said, he may know something and not realize its importance."

"What do you want from me?"

"You probably know Ben better than anyone. What can you tell me about him?"

Schneider pursed his lips. "You wouldn't think it to look at him now, but during the war he was a ring-tailed hellion!"

"What? Ben Kepler?"

Schneider grinned. "He was the champion no-holds-barred fighter in the company. Lick any man of 'em. Includin' me."

Reb was astonished. "Are we talking about the same man?"

"Did you ever see Ben with his shirt off?"

"No . . ."

"He's all muscle and full of scars. 'Course, he's older now and wears specs." Schneider looked out over the parade ground. "I recollect them days, seein' him lead the company on a hell-for-leather chase agin the Unions. . . ." He sighed. "We was young and wild then. Those times ain't gonna come again. . . ."

"Have you any idea where Ben went from here?"

"He didn't say."

"Was he armed?"

"He had a pistol in his belt, yes."

Reb asked, "Does he know how to use it?"

Schneider looked surprised. " 'Course he knows how to use it! I told you, we was with Forrest! Every man was an expert. If they had give Forrest more men, we woulda won the goddamn war!"

11

On the lonely ride back to Wakefield, he thought about the marshal's daughter, Lorrie. Other men his age were settling down, raising families. But he was not able to fit himself into that company . . . yet. In his occupation he had no business asking a woman to share the worries. Probably none would, anyhow. How many times had he heard it said, "There is always someone better or quicker than you"?

But all that aside, it was pleasant to let his imagination soar, with her in mind. It also eased the miles.

In Wakefield he put the sorrel horse in the stable and walked to the jail office, reporting to an astonished Marshal Winters what Sergeant Schneider had told him.

"Is it possible Ben shot them two men?"

"Of course it's possible. The mystery is *why*. Why, after working for Chartis all those years, would he suddenly shoot him?"

"Nothing makes sense."

"And Aiken, too. Everyone seemed to like Aiken."

The marshal selected a cigar and rolled it in his fingers absently. "But somebody was after Kepler—shot his horse. Pro'ly the same one shot at you."

"I don't doubt it."

"I sent the details about Kepler down to Carter and Ganz Siding and up to Vetter. I wish to hell we had a telegraph here. I keep hearin' it's coming, but so is Christmas."

Reb paced the room restlessly. "I'd like to know more

about Kepler but there's no one here in town who really knew him. I've a hunch the answer is in his past."

"You better go back to Hayes, then, and talk to that sergeant."

"First, I'm going down to Ganz. The train stops there, right?"

"If he went there, he's in Frisco by now. Or St. Louie."

Reb shrugged. "Got to do what I can."

He took the stagecoach to Carter, and described Kepler to the station master, who shook his head, saying he'd seen half a dozen who could be the wanted man.

It was another three days to Ganz Siding, a sketchy little burg that was strung out along the railroad, dusty and forlorn. It was a water stop, but there was a siding. Apparently, ranchers in the south drove there after their roundups.

No one he talked to had seen Kepler—for sure. The man he described could be one of hundreds. If only he'd had a photograph. . . . It was like finding a toothpick in a barley field.

He spent a day in Ganz and took the next stage north feeling discouraged. Had Kepler given him the slip for good? It seemed likely.

When Reb returned to Wakefield, Winters had no news for him. Jim had gone to the cabin and returned with the saddle, without incident. He had also brought back Kepler's saddle. If Kepler came and claimed it, it was his, otherwise the county would auction it off . . . after a decent interval.

Winter was coming. The first rain came and went in a day, and Reb rode to Fort Hayes when the sun came out again. Sergeant Schneider was surprised to see him. "You find Ben yet?"

"No. No sign of him."

They talked in Schneider's quarters, a room off one of the barracks' buildings. It was Spartan, containing a double bunk, two chairs, a stove for heat, and a bit of carpet on the floor. There were no pictures on the walls and no curtains on the single window.

Reb explained that he had no reason to believe Ben Kepler had shot anyone, but he felt the answer to the mystery might lie in Ben's past. Could Schneider help him in that regard?

Schneider shrugged lightly as he loaded a pipe. "Ben comes from a little town in Oklahoma Territory, Anders. Prob'ly five hunnerd people in all. His parents are dead, but I think there's kin still around-about. Ben had a brother, killed in the war, and I'm sure he had a sister. I don't know anything about her."

"Was he ever married?"

"Yes, a long time ago." The sergeant shook his head. "I got no idea what become of her. He married right after the war, and I lost track of him for years."

"You and he were in the Confederate Army. . . ."

Schneider nodded, smiling. "I guess I got army in m'blood. Ben didn't. Soon's Bob Lee give up, he took off for parts unknown. I didn't see him again for years. When I seen him again, he wasn't married no more, and he didn't want to talk about it." He scratched a match and lit the pipe.

"When I told you I was investigating a murder and mentioned Ben Kepler's name, you seemed to indicate that Ben was not one to shoot anyone."

Schneider was silent a moment, puffing blue smoke. "Let's say I don't think Ben would shoot somebody unless he had one hell of a good reason. I seen him shoot plenty during the war . . . but that's something else, ain't it?"

Reb smiled. "I've never been in a war, but I would think so."

When he returned to Wakefield, there was a note waiting for him from Klara Chartis. She consented to a visit from him. It was like an invitation from the queen, Reb thought. "Come to the palace and wear your Sunday suit."

He told Winters what he had learned and suggested Winters write the county sheriff asking for information about the Keplers. Winters got a letter off at once.

* * *

He met Mrs. Chartis in her home, a red-brick building set back from the street, undoubtedly the finest house in Wakefield. For the visit, Reb had his boots shined and did not wear the .44 pistol.

The door was opened by a Chinese servant who bowed to him and bade him enter. "Missy say you sit down . . ." He showed Reb to a small ornate room to the right of the door and disappeared.

He returned in several minutes, "You come come . . ."

Reb followed the slight figure into a sitting room. Mrs. Chartis was standing by a fireplace and waved the servant out. "You are Mr. Wiley?"

"Yes . . ."

"Please sit down." She was dressed in black and gray, a dress with a large amount of black lace, to the throat. She was not a big woman, but not fragile-looking, as the marshal had led him to believe. He sat gingerly on a gilt chair.

"I am sorry I was not able to see you sooner," she said in a husky voice. "The tragedy was almost more than I could bear. . . ." Her hands fluttered. "A terrible shock, as I am sure you understand." She sighed deeply. "I don't know how I can help you. I had nothing to do with the operation of the store. . . ."

"Did your husband have any enemies, Mrs. Chartis?"

"None that I am aware of. And neither did poor Mr. Aiken. I have been talking to my attorney, Mr. Lisser, concerning selling our property in Wakefield, all of it, including the store. I would like to go east, to get away from these terrible memories. I am not sleeping properly, even now."

"When do you intend to do that, sell the store?"

"I've not yet made up my mind." She toyed with a bit of cambric handkerchief. "When I first came here, this was such a peaceful place. But now, it is all changed, and I fear for my life whenever I go outside."

"You feel you have something to fear?"

She looked at him with wide eyes. "Murder has come very close to me, young man! How should I feel?" She fluttered the bit of cloth, moving restlessly. "There is an evil—some thing—out there." She waved her arm vaguely. "Has the marshal found my husband's killer?" She did not wait for an answer. "I once went for long drives, but now I dare not leave the safety of the house—unless I am well guarded."

"Did your husband discuss his problems with you?"

"Problems? What do you mean?"

"There must have been problems in the operation of the store or perhaps in his handling of other properties. . . ."

She sighed. "He kept business affairs to himself. I had no training in that direction. I had full confidence in his decisions."

The small Chinese man came in silently with a silver tray containing a silver pot and two china teacups. He laid the tray on a small table and withdrew like a wraith, closing the door again. Mrs. Chartis seemed not to notice.

Reb said, "Was your husband in the habit of working late at the store?"

"Yes, he often went there or stayed there in the evenings. He kept no regular hours."

"And he had no enemies?"

She looked at him sharply. "None that I know about. Why do you harp on that?"

"He had one, Mrs. Chartis. Someone shot him."

She seemed about to burst into tears. She crossed the room, holding the handkerchief to her face, turning her back. Reb rose, wondering if he should go. There was obviously very little she could tell him. He moved toward the door, and she regained her poise, holding herself stiffly.

"Please forgive me . . . I am still battling . . . this . . ."

"I won't intrude any longer, Mrs. Chartis." Reb opened the door and went out. The Chinese man was waiting by the front door. He bowed, opened the door, and closed it as Reb went out into the air. He had gained very little. Chartis obviously kept her in the dark concerning business.

Marshal Winters thought so, too. "I didn't think she'd tell you anything. She don't know nothing. What you gonna do now?"

"Have supper," Reb said. "Then I'll have a glass of beer and worry about where Ben Kepler is."

Winters took off his hat and stretched. "I'd go with you, but this is Jim's day off so I gotta make the rounds." He stood up and put the hat on.

12

The gold leaf on the door window read: THOMAS LISSER ATTY AT LAW. ENTER.

Reb opened the door and saw Mr. Lisser seated at a desk across the small room. He was alone, writing in a notebook. Behind him were law books, shelves of them in black bindings. Two other tables in the room were piled with folders and loose papers; the room smelled of tobacco. Lisser looked up and nodded. "Come in . . ."

Reb closed the door behind him, and Lisser said, "You're the one who's working with Bill Winters. . . . Your name's Wiley."

"That's right." Reb sat in a chair facing the desk.

"What can I do for you, Mr. Wiley?"

"I'm told you're Mrs. Chartis's lawyer."

"Yes . . . Have you been to see her?"

"Yes, I have. And learned very little."

Lisser made a face. "She doesn't know anything to tell. Homer Chartis never told anyone anything he didn't have to. He was a close-mouthed penny-pincher. But I suppose you know all that by now."

"How did you know my name?"

Lisser smiled thinly. "It's all over town who you are, sir. Did you know people are making bets about you?"

"Bets?" Reb stared at the lawyer. Lisser was thin and sharp-nosed. He dressed like an undertaker, and had long, thin fingers, white as paper. He wore specs and looked over them at his visitor.

"Yes. Bets on how long you'll last—against the killer of Chartis and Aiken."

Reb was astonished, and Lisser seemed to enjoy his discomfiture. "They think I'll be bushwhacked?"

"Apparently."

"And did you bet, too, Mr. Lisser?"

He was further surprised when Lisser rummaged in a desk drawer and brought out a square of green paper. He passed it across the desk. "That cost me one dollar."

Reb frowned. The card was written in ink: *Saturday 12 Oct.* He looked at the skinny lawyer. "You think I'll be killed next Saturday?"

Lisser laughed shortly. "I picked a date out of thin air. So did everyone else. Half the town is in on this."

"That means you think the killer is still in town."

"No," Lisser corrected. "It means it's merely something to bet on. No hard feelings."

Reb shrugged. "What about her property, Mr. Lisser? Is she going to sell and get out or not?"

"She can't make up her mind. She's a woman who never had property or a measure of wealth before, and she doesn't know what to do with it—so she does nothing. You saw how she is."

"Yes . . ."

"So I go along with her moods." Lisser smiled. "If she wants to sell out, fine. If not, fine." He spread his hands. "That's all I can tell you."

Reb left, still surprised about the lottery. Would some citizen shoot him because he had that date? It made him feel itchy. Did the marshal know about the betting?

He did. Winters said, "I didn't tell you because I didn't want you to feel like the turkey who's waitin' for Thanksgiving. It don't mean nothing. Some bartender started it. Them fools bets on anything. I seen 'em bet on the exact time the stage rolls in and stops at the depot."

"I'd rather they'd bet on that in future."

"Folks don't always do what you want—which I am sure you have figgered out by now. You best ignore the whole thing. And while you're ignorin' it, my daughter Lorrie's birthday is tomorra. So you are invited to supper. I'm havin'a woman come in to cook it for us. Lorrie is gonna be twenty-two."

"I'm delighted to be asked. Thank you."

"Come to the house about sundown and wear a clean shirt. Lorrie's a fussy kid."

"Does she let you wear your hat in the house?"

The marshal sighed. "That ain't all she won't let me do. She was a little girl about two weeks ago—and now she's twenty-two. I can't get used to it."

On the way back to the hotel, Reb stopped at the Chartis store and shopped for a present. What would a young woman like? Well, of course if it was a present, she'd say she liked it. . . .

The store didn't provide much choice. There were almost no luxury articles, no frills or fripperies. He talked to clerk Axel Lynch, explaining his mission, and Axel suggested a fan. "We got some nice ivory carved fans in not long ago."

"Let's see them."

Axel pulled out a large velvet-lined case containing six fans and laid it on the counter. "Ain't these pretty?"

"They sure are." They were very decorative, highly carved from thin ivory; they opened and closed, held together by silken threads.

The clerk said, "If she don't like one of them, she don't like mashed potatoes."

"I agree with you," Reb said. "How do I wrap it up?"

"We got some white tissue paper—where the hell is it? Oh here . . ." Axel rummaged in a cabinet, brought out a roll of paper and cut off a square. He deftly wrapped one of the fans and tied it with a bit of red ribbon. "How's that investigation goin', Mr. Reb?"

"It's poking along." He counted out the money and pushed it across the counter. "Have you got one of those little green cards?"

Axel looked uncomfortable. "I had one, but the date gone past."

Reb laughed. "Thanks for the wrapping." He took the present and went out. At the hotel he had a bath for the occasion, had his hair trimmed by a barber, bought a new shirt, and wore clean jeans and polished boots, smiling as he examined himself in the wavy mirror. He was dressed for church.

He slid into the buckskin coat as dusk approached, and wrapped the cartridge belt about his lean hips, with the .44 in the greased holster. He dared not go naked in the streets, not after hearing about the bets. There might easily be as much as a hundred dollars in the kitty, and men had killed each other for less. He would leave the pistol in the marshal's hallway when he got there.

He thought about flowers when he went downstairs, and asked the clerk. But there was no shop in town; not in hundreds of miles, the clerk said. "Women out here in the sticks don't expect no flowers . . . less'n you picks 'em wild out on the prairie. . . ."

Maybe it was just as well. If he brought her flowers, she might think he considered himself a suitor.

He smiled as he walked to the livery stable. He might like very much to be . . . She was easily the most beautiful woman in the territory, and probably had brains to boot.

Jed Urshel saddled a roan horse for him and loaned him a poncho. It was beginning to drizzle. "Don't git that there pretty present wet."

"Thanks, I won't."

Marshal Winters lived at the far end of town; he knew the house though he'd never been inside it. The drizzle increased, and there was no one on the street. He rode directly into the marshal's open stable and slid down.

Winters was watching for him and opened the back door of the house. "Come in out of the wet, boy. . . ."

The house was redolent with food smells, promising much. He followed Winters in through the kitchen, where an aproned woman smiled at him, busy over pots and pans on the large black wood stove.

Lorrie was in the parlor, wearing a pink and white dress,

and her hair was fluffed, not like he'd seen it first; he thought it made her look even more beautiful. Winters was beaming and obviously proud.

"Will you lookit her? I seen the time I could hold her in one hand! With her little screwed-up face—"

"Oh, goodness, Daddy! Stop it!" She smiled at Reb. "I'm glad you could come, Mr. Wiley. Will you have some punch? I made it myself."

"My friends call me Reb."

"Reb? Why is that?" She ladled punch into a glass and handed it to him.

"I don't know. They always have. I think my uncle started it when I was a little tad."

He pulled the present from inside his coat. "This is for you. . . ."

"For me!" Her eyes widened.

"It's your birthday."

"What is it?" Winters asked. "A package of macaroni?"

She gave him a frown and tore off the paper. "It's a fan!" She looked closer. "It's ivory! How wonderful!" She laughed and spread it out. "It's beautiful!" She fluttered it close to her cheek in a seductive manner, and Reb's heart beat faster. He nodded as she thanked him, not trusting himself to say the right words.

The woman in the kitchen saved him. She came to the door. "Y'all want to eat now?"

"We're having boned leg of lamb," Lorrie announced. "It's a favorite dish of Mrs. Massey, and not easy to prepare on a wood stove."

Winters and Reb clapped as Mrs. Massey brought in the platter. She put it in front of Winters, who stood with a long, gleaming knife. "Pass me your plates, you first, Lorrie. . . ."

There was also homemade bread, hot from the oven, carrots and limas and apple pie, when they were ready. Winters regaled them with stories about Lorrie when she was very young, occasionally to her discomfit.

"Do you have to tell him *that*, Daddy!"

Mrs. Massey brought in freshly ground coffee, and Reb felt he had seldom dined as well.

Her father gave her jewelry, a necklace and matching bracelet with small pearls, which she exclaimed over and hugged him for. Reb sighed to himself; if Winters had not been present, would she have hugged him, too?

The evening came to an end with brandy, served to each by Lorrie. She declared it to be the best twenty-second birthday she had ever had.

13

The rain still held off when Reb rode the roan back to the livery. Jed was asleep in the back, so Reb unsaddled the horse and hung the saddle and bridle on a peg, draped the poncho over them and went to the door, settling the hat on his head. The drizzle was feathery, and the distant lights had haloes. . . .

When he took a step from the shadows of the doorway, he felt the tug at his collar—then heard the shot. The bullet tore through the leather coat at the neck; he thought he could feel its passing. He jumped back into the deep shadows as a second shot slammed into a wooden stall behind him, and this time he saw the orange muzzle blast. The sniper was on the roof of a low building across the street, probably a hundred or more feet away.

Pistol in hand, Reb ran across the dark street; no shot came. There was no opening between buildings here, and he had to run past several stores to gain entrance to the alley behind them. And he knew, by the time he got there, the sniper would have disappeared.

He walked the length of the alley and back, pistol ready, and met no one. It was late; most folks were long ago in bed. Probably the poor light had saved him.

So he had been followed. The sniper knew where he had gone and probably waited for him to return. He had picked a time and place where no one would be about. But unfortunately for the sniper, he had picked a time when accurate shooting was most difficult. And the fact that Reb had been moving probably forced the sniper to hurry the shot.

Was this the same one who had fired at him in the hills? Probably. And fired from a distance. Did that mean anything?

Reb kept to the shadows on the way to the hotel, but he did not expect another attempt. Apparently this particular sniper did not want to come face-to-face with him . . . in pistol range.

Unless all the cards were stacked his way.

Marshal Winters was annoyed to hear about the ambush attempt. "You figger it's the same feller?"

Reb's eyes opened wide. "I hope to hell I don't have two snipers after me!"

The other nodded seriously and scratched a match for his morning cigar. "Don't do nothing the same way twice." He peered at Reb over the flame. "Why is he shootin' at you? Are you gettin' close to something—and don't know it?"

"I suppose that's possible."

"Of course, maybe he jus' don't like your looks."

"That must be it." Reb sighed and went to the door, staring at the dusty street. He'd have to go by the shoemaker's shop. The sniper had ruined the collar of the buckskin coat. Maybe the shoemaker could stitch it up. He hated to throw away a good coat. . . .

He watched a light wagon, pulled by two black mules, turn the corner and come toward him. An older, hunched-up man sat on the seat with loose reins in his hands. He stopped the wagon in front of the office and squinted at Reb from under a shapeless hat. "You the marshal?"

Reb shook his head. "He's inside."

The old man climbed down over the wheel and stretched both arms out. "I come a long way b'fore breakfast." He limped into the office and stared at Winters. "Hello, Marshal. My name's Jake Reiss and I want t'report a robbery."

"Was you the one robbed?"

" 'Course I am!"

"Where did this here crime take place?"

" 'Bout a day's ride out on the Hamelin road. Sombitch helt me up and took thirty dollars, hard money and all my airtights. Took m'canteen, too."

Winters dutifully wrote down the particulars. "What'd this feller look like?"

"Well, he was bigger'n me, wore specs, and was ridin' a army horse. I seen the brand on it. Otherwise he looked like anybody else."

"How old would you say he was?" Reb asked.

Jake's brows came together and he chewed his lip. "Maybe fifty . . ."

"Not a young'un!" The marshal pushed his hat back. "You sure?"

" 'Course I'm sure. I sat there a-starin' at him, didn't I? The sombitch tol' me t'git offen the wagon seat, then he throwed my stuff out on the ground. Made me turn out m'pockets and searched the goddamn wagon. Took ever' penny I had!"

"And where'd he go?"

"He didn't go nowhere! Told me to git! Sat there on his goddamn horse and watched me go. That's the last I seen him, sittin' there."

"All right, Mr. Reiss," Winters said, "we'll look into this. Where you gonna be?"

Reiss shrugged thin shoulders. "I dunno. I got some odds'n ends in the wagon. I could put up at the hotel for a night'r two if I sell 'em." He moved to the door. "First goddamn time I ever been robbed! You catch this sombitch, Marshal." He went out and climbed on the wagon.

Reb watched the old man turn the wagon around in the street and head back the way he had come. He said, "You think it's Kepler?"

"I'd bet the farm on it, and both mules. We ain't had a robbery like that in years around here. I don't remember the last one." He took his hat off and sighed. "Fifty-year-old holdup man who wears specs. Hell's fire, it got to be Kepler."

"Umm-hum. He took food and a canteen. That was probably the reason for the robbery."

"Which means he don't want to come into town."

"I think so, too."

Winters put the hat on again. "Half the folks in town knows 'im, that's for sure." He squinted at Reb. "So he's hanging around."

"Yes. But what for?" Reb frowned at the street.

"To shoot you?"

Reb made a face. He turned. "If he's trying to shoot me because of the Chartis-Aiken case, why doesn't he shoot you, too? You know as much as I do."

Winters pulled out a desk drawer and put his feet up. "Maybe he don't know that."

"Just the same, don't go home the same way twice."

Marshal Winters received two letters, a week apart. One was from the county sheriff at Ganz Siding. To the best of his knowledge, Kepler had not been seen in that area.

The second letter was from the Pawnee County sheriff, Oklahoma Territory, concerning Benjamin Kepler. The man in question, the sheriff wrote, was probably not in the county, but his uncle, Norton Kepler, still lived in Anders. Norton was the brother of Ben's father. Norton and his wife had two children, both living in Anders.

Ben's father and mother were both dead. They had three children: Ben, a daughter, and a younger son who had been killed in the war. Ben and his sister, Katherine, had left Anders many years before. The sheriff had no idea where they were. He was sorry, but that was all he could tell Winters.

The sheriff at Vetter did not reply.

But none of this was much help.

John Franken searched through boxes and files, he told the marshal, and could find no file on the man who had been fired years ago by Chartis. "It probably been burnt with the trash."

"It wasn't much of a possibility anyhow," Reb said. "Too long ago."

Winters had Deputy Jim gather up a posse and ride out on the Hamelin road—though he had no jurisdiction there—looking for Kepler or any evidence of his passing. The marshal doubted they would find anything, but at least he was doing something that might look promising in the weekly.

The posse returned late that same day, arriving in town after dark, one horse carrying double. They had met someone, Jim told the marshal and Reb, who had run from them on sight. When they chased him, he opened fire and hit one of the horses. He had also nicked a posseman in the lower leg and had gotten clean away.

"We had to shoot the horse," Jim said. "The hombre must of knowed the country good because he ducked away and we never did catch his trail again."

Reb asked, "Do you think it was Kepler?"

Jim shrugged. "I guess so. He sure run like hell when he seen us. But we never got a close look at him."

When Jim had gone, Reb said, "He's hanging around close."

Winters grinned. "That's because he got one of them green tickets on you."

"Very funny."

Reb walked down the street to the shoemaker's shop and discussed the buckskin coat with the owner, who thought the collar could be stitched to look presentable. "I'll put in a patch. . . . It ain't going to look like new, but it'll get by."

Reb left the coat with him and returned to the office. Jim had put his horse in the stable and was showing the marshal on a map where they had met the stranger.

"It was about eight, nine mile from town," Jim said. "We was off the road a little bit, and we got to thinkin' afterward that maybe we come close to where he was campin' out."

"Sounds likely," Winters agreed.

But neither Jim nor any of the possemen was able to say for sure the man they had seen was Kepler. None had gotten a good enough look at him. He might be any drifter—there were plenty of them around. If a drifter were suddenly flushed out of his camp by a group of armed men, he might well run like hell.

There were ominous stories about men who had been lynched by mobs of cattlemen who had later learned they'd stretched the wrong man.

If the man Jim and the posse had seen was Kepler, why was he hanging around? Was he the sniper?

Reb turned it all over in his mind. It was possible that Ben had shot his own horse in the cabin corral . . . to make it look as if someone was after him. But that theory had a large drawback. It meant that Ben had to foot it all the way to Fort Hayes. Also, he had seen a horseman, after he'd found Ben's dead horse. That horseman had fired at him. So it was unlikely that Ben was the sniper. Wasn't it? Nobody could be in several places at once.

He swore under his breath. What the hell was the truth of all this? There were always too many questions and terrible answers.

He decided to go back to Homer Chartis and dig into his past. Maybe something would come to light.

Marshal Winters thought it a good idea. "*If* you can find someone who knew him before he come to Wakefield. You got to remember that ever' now and then a crime comes along that ain't got no solution. This could be one of 'em."

"That's not what I want to hear."

Winters sniffed. "Try George Gibbons. He knew Chartis better'n anyone else in town—'cept his wife. Anyway, I seen 'em with their heads together many a time."

It was a good suggestion. Reb called on the council president in his office over the hardware store. A middle-aged secretary, Mr. Loomis, according to the small hand-lettered sign on his desk, listened to his request gravely, entered Gibbons's office and came out in a moment.

"Please go in, Mr. Wiley."

George Gibbons looked exactly the same, wearing a dark

gray frock coat, immaculate shirt, and black cravat. His handshake was just as soft, and his voice well modulated—Reb found it impossible to think of the man angry. Gibbons indicated a chair. "Please sit down, Reb. What can I do for you? Are you making progress with the case?"

Reb sat. "Not much. It's a tangle . . . so far. But what I need is more information about Homer Chartis."

"Ahhhh." Gibbons put his fingertips together. "Chartis—you mean his early life? Before he came here?"

"Yes."

"Well, let me see . . . I know that he came from St. Louis. I'm not sure he was born there. I believe he had family or an ex-wife—yes, I'm sure he was married before he met Klara. Homer was close-mouthed, you know. I don't know why they separated."

"Was he in business in St. Louis?"

"Oh yes. He owned a mercantile store in partnership with someone else—I don't know who."

"Do you know what the store was called?"

Gibbons frowned at his fingers. "I'm afraid not, but it was probably both names—like Smith and Jones Mercantile. That's common practice. And Chartis is a rather unusual name, so possibly you can trace it."

"Yes. Can you tell me anything about the first wife . . . her name, for instance?"

"I think it was Mary, or Marie. . . . He mentioned her once to me, a long time ago. I got the impression they were married only a short time."

"Do you know when he married Klara?"

"They met in Vetter. Joe Aiken told me that."

Reb was surprised. "What was Aiken doing in Vetter?"

Gibbons smiled. "Chartis was there looking for a place to start another business. He and Aiken were together by then. I believe they met in Kansas City. Aiken had a background in retail. Evidently that was their common interest. Joe told me that he came south here to Wakefield and advised Chartis that Wakefield was ideal and there was even a building available."

"Then Chartis married Klara and came south."

"Yes. Did you know that Chartis bought the building from John Franken?"

"Yes, Franken told me. He also said that Chartis had a store in Vetter, with his father."

Gibbons shook his head. "That was a story that Chartis put out. Not a grain of truth in it. Chartis hated to have anyone know his affairs or business, so he put up smoke screens like that Vetter store story. He was a secretive man."

Reb rubbed his chin. "I find it curious that Joe Aiken stayed with him so long. From what I've heard, they were very different people."

"Yes, that is odd. Apparently there was a bond between them—I can't define it, but I'm sure no one else would have lasted half as long with Chartis."

"They met in Kansas City . . . ?"

"Yes. Joe told me he was at loose ends, doing this and that. He met Chartis through a business acquaintance. Chartis was married then, having problems with his wife."

"Problems?"

Gibbons raised his tailored shoulders an inch. "He never explained them, and I didn't ask."

Reb smiled. "You knew quite a bit, Mr. Gibbons. I really thank you."

"I hope it helps with the case. Chartis was a curious man, and not well liked by his employees—I suppose you've heard that."

"Yes. Did you like him, Mr. Gibbons?"

The other took a long breath. "I try not to judge my fellows. . . . I'm a churchman, Reb. I will say that Chartis was always most interested in money, rather than people."

"But you liked Aiken?"

"Oh yes. He was a very amiable sort. But never talked about his employer."

Reb got up. "You've been very helpful. . . ."

"If I think of anything else, I'll get word to you at once."

"Thank you again."

Reb went to the door, and Gibbons said, "There's one thing more—Chartis once mentioned that he had a relative in Carter. Perhaps you can ask Mrs. Chartis about him."

14

Marshal Winters took off his hat and listened carefully as Reb outlined what he had learned. He nodded slowly. "I heard that story, too, about Chartis havin' a store in Vetter. So it ain't true?"

"Apparently not. No one ever checked it?"

"Well, it was three or four hunnerd mile away and fifteen years ago. Folks is not all that fascinated by a store, you know. What you going to do next?"

"Get you to write to St. Louis. Try to find out who Chartis's partner was."

"That's a long time ago to be comin' here to shoot him."

Reb shook his head. "I doubt if his long-time-ago partner shot him. But he might be able to give us some information. And I think I'll have to go to Carter again."

"You're wearing out the road." Winters put his hat on. "Lorrie is talkin' about going to school again. What the hell gets into women's heads?"

"What does she want to study?"

"She's talkin' about being a teacher—maybe a professor. How many women professors are they anyhow?"

Reb shook his head. "No idea. When is she going?"

"Not for a while."

"Will you write to St. Louis in your official capacity? Ask the law there about Chartis's store. We want to know his partner's name and anything they can tell us about him."

"Yeah, right away." Winters sighed. "I'll get Lorrie to write it. She got a nice hand. I'll sign it."

* * *

The editor and owner of the Wakefield *Democrat* was Nigel Trager, a lean, graying man who apparently never combed his hair and customarily wore a buttoned-up vest over his shirt, with pencils sticking out of the pockets. He left his coat on a nail in the littered office.

As Reb asked him about Chartis, he fiddled with a silver watch chain. "Our only dealings with Chartis were for ads in the paper. In all those years, I never formally met Chartis—was never introduced to him, at any rate. He was never in this office."

"So you dealt with Mr. Aiken?"

"Yes. All our dealings were with Joe Aiken, the store manager." He smiled thinly. "I heard you were on the case, Mr. Wiley." He glanced at the .44 on Reb's hip. "Forgive me, but your reputation has preceded you."

Reb smiled in return. "Don't believe too much of the gossip, Mr. Trager. Do you also have one of those little green cards?"

Trager's eyes twinkled. "Yes, one or two." He paused. "I understand you were shot at not long ago, near the livery."

"How did you hear that?" He and Winters had not made it public.

"We're newspaper people here, Mr. Wiley. We hear things—even those that are hushed up."

"I hope you won't print it. . . ."

Trager took off his specs and rubbed his eyes briefly. "The incident hasn't much news value. There was no resolution." He put the specs on and looked over them. "No one is able to collect on the betting pool."

"Too bad," Reb said acidly. "I suppose you talked to the shoemaker. . . ."

"Yes."

"What can you tell me about Joseph Aiken? I've been told he met Chartis in Kansas City."

"Yes, I believe that is so. He said once that Chartis wanted to come west—something about believing in the future. He would open a large store, the biggest in the territory—and I guess he did.''

''And Aiken became his manager.''

''Aiken could show a lot of experience in retail selling, yes. He said he'd been in it all his life, and his father before him. I'm sure that impressed Chartis. And he was a good manager—or he'd never have lasted so long in the store.''

''You didn't like Chartis much. . . .''

''No one did.'' Trager shrugged slightly. ''But I didn't know him, as I said, we never met. I only know what others told me.''

''Aiken had been married, but he wasn't when he came here. And he remained single for those fifteen years or more.''

''You're not married, either, Mr. Wiley.''

Reb smiled. ''But I'm younger than Aiken was, and he had a better job, home nights. Not so much running about the landscape. Was there any town talk about his being single?''

''I suppose so. We're not much interested in gossip here, except for our regular gossip column, of course. I have no idea why he never married again. We didn't discuss it. I have no idea what happened to his first wife. They may have separated and not divorced. Divorce is not common, as you know.''

''What can you tell me about enemies? Did Aiken have any?''

''That would be a guess on my part. I have no way of knowing. I do know that he was well liked, and he even made excuses for Chartis. Many in town that I've talked to think he was killed by a stranger.''

''We don't think that's likely.''

''But you don't know who did it? Or who did both?''

Reb nodded. ''The murders may never be solved. There's always that.''

Trager shrugged again. ''Many aren't.''

* * *

Reb got his leather coat from the shoemaker and was very pleased. The man had done a careful job of patching and stitching; the harm the bullet had done could hardly be seen.

He donned the coat and went to the depot to buy a ticket for Carter. The next stage was due in a day.

In the office he said to Winters, "If Chartis had a relative in Carter, I want to talk to him."

"Maybe he won't talk to you," the marshal said. "You've got no jurisdiction."

"I'll cross that creek when I come to it."

"I'd make you a deputy, but the badge ain't worth a handful of cow flop in Carter."

"I d'want to be bound by it anyway. Without the badge, I can play it by my own rules."

Winters sighed deeply. "You got no proper respect for the law."

"I respect it to the skies—so long as it's on my side. If it isn't, it can take its chances."

"I rest my case," Winters said.

Reb was sitting in the waiting room when the stage and six pulled into the yard. The driver and shotgun went in for lunch while the horses were changed and passenger luggage loaded.

He climbed aboard with three others, a drummer, a lad of about fourteen, and a man who looked like a drifter but who said he was a discharged cavalryman and had gotten out after his second hitch.

"Goddamn army's a pain in the ass," he said to anyone who would listen. "Allus marchin' somewhere, and if it ain't rainin', it's too damn hot."

"What you aimed at now?" the drummer asked him.

"I learnt the blacksmith trade. That's why I stayed in the second time. Now I can get a job wi'out no damn reveille."

They eyed Reb and his .44, and the drummer asked him what he did.

"I'm a deputy marshal in Wakefield," he told them, and they all nodded and changed the subject. Reb pulled the seldom-worn hat off his back, tipped it over his eyes, and relaxed, rolling with the motion of the coach.

It began to rain lightly as they left town, and the mild storm stayed with them to the first way station.

The rain pursued them to Carter, making the journey uncomfortable, especially when the wind drove the icy rain into the coach. It had no glass, only canvas curtains that turned very little aside.

In Carter he visited the town law, a deputy sheriff; the sheriff was out making political rounds, it being close to election time. But the deputy was not helpful. "There ain't no Chartis in town that I know of. Whyn't you try the paper?"

The newsweekly was the *Ledger*, and the editor shook his head. "Chartis? Only one I ever heard of was the one got shot in Wakefield."

"Can you think of anyone else in town who might know?"

"Yes, there're two or three who have been here longest. You might ask them. . . ."

With directions, Reb found an older woman who said she had known the man who built the first building in town. But she did not know the name Chartis. She directed him to an older man who was deaf. Reb wrote out the name on a paper, but the old man shook his head.

There was no one in Carter by that name. Was George Gibbons unintentionally repeating another of Chartis's smoke screens? It certainly seemed like it.

Reluctantly he took the next stage back to Wakefield and reported to Marshal Winters that it had been a fool's errand. Chartis was probably the only one of that name west of the Missouri.

Winters puffed his cigar, feet up on a desk drawer. "Hell, there ain't no Chartis anywhere. Not in St. Louis, not in Carter, and not here in Wakefield, 'cept for Klara, and she don't really count."

Reb sighed. "I expect I'll have to talk to her again. . . ."

"You won't learn nothing. That's a fool's errand, too. She'll flutter around, and you just be wastin' your time."

"I'm afraid you're right."

That evening at the hotel he wrote a note, asking Mrs. Chartis for a few moments of her time. He had the clerk send it by a delivery boy.

She sent a message back by the boy, to his surprise. She would see him the next day at eleven in the morning, if that was convenient. . . .

He rode again to the red-brick house, left his horse in the stable, with the .44 and belt hanging on the horn, and the same Chinese man opened the door. Reb was expected and ushered into the same sitting room.

"You sit, please . . ." The man disappeared silently.

Klara Chartis came into the room in a few moments. She seemed much more contained, Reb thought. Her grief was under control.

"What is it, Mr. Wiley?"

She was wearing a dark blue dress under a gold-colored silken wrapper that looked very elegant. She did not sit, but stood by the fireplace. Her face seemed unnaturally pale, and he wondered if she was heavily powdered. The light was dim, and she stood ten feet away, holding a pair of spectacles as if she had been reading.

He said, "I am told that your husband had a relative in Carter. Can you tell me if that is true?"

Her brows went up in surprise. "In Carter? No, not to my knowledge."

"Did he have *any* living relatives?"

She frowned, twisting the spectacles. "Yes, he had an older brother, but I have no idea where he is. He and Homer did not get on well."

"Did you ever meet him?"

"No, never." She shook her head slightly. "My husband seldom spoke of him. Apparently, they had quarreled from birth. And he was much older than Homer."

"Do you recall his name?"

"Oh yes. It was Willis."

"And there was no other family?"

"No. None."

"So I assume, Mrs. Chartis, that the brother was not mentioned in your husband's will?"

"No, he was not. I believe Homer thought of him as a stranger. They had never gotten on as boys, and Homer never asked Willis to go into business with him."

"Do you know if they had a really serious quarrel, enough for them to become enemies?"

She thought for a moment, staring over his head. "No, I do not. Of course, all this happened before I met Homer. I'm sure you realize—"

"Yes. But I get the impression from what you say that the enmity went deep."

"I believe it did."

Reb rose. "Thank you, Mrs. Chartis."

He rode back slowly, thinking over what she had said. Had she told him the truth? Did she really know so little about her husband's affairs?

15

"An interesting possibility," Reb said to Winters. "Did one brother kill another?"

"Cain and Abel?"

"We can't rule it out."

Winters pulled his hat down lower. "But where's the other brother?"

"I don't know. Neither does she."

"Space," Winters said, taking off the hat.

"What?"

"The way to avoid arrest is to put a hell of a lot of space between you and the nearest sheriff. If Chartis's brother did the shooting, he is on a boat to China by now, telling some female horrendous lies. And if you write that out, I will sign it." He put the hat on again.

"All right, Mr. Oracle, why did he kill Aiken?"

"Just so you would stand in the middle of the goddamn room and ast me a bunch of damn-fool questions that nobody knows the answers to. What's an oracle?"

"A big mouth. You figure it's the brother?"

Winters sighed. "Pro'ly not."

The same afternoon, Winters received a note from John Franken at the store. Ben Kepler's safe combination had been discovered. Did the marshal want to be present when it was opened?

He sent back a note. He did. He frowned at Reb. "They never said they was a safe."

"And I never thought to ask."

Franken met them in his office. He was in a brown suit and cravat, with brown shoes and a brown smile. He got up from behind his desk, greeted them, and led them into Kepler's office.

"We found the combination scratched on a pewter ashtray. We didn't notice it before because it was covered with grit and ashes. We had a handyman in here to clean, and he noticed it . . . brought it to me."

Winters said, "You didn't mention a safe."

"Well, it was locked." Franken shrugged. "Nothing you could do about it then. Ben had the combination changed, so we didn't have a record of it."

The safe was standing in the middle of the room. It had been hidden by a cabinet before. Reb said, "Let's open it."

Franken nodded and knelt in front of it with a paper in his hand. He twisted the dial slowly, carefully matching the numbers. He grasped the handle and looked up at them.

"Here it is. . . ." He opened the door.

The safe had a shelf and a lockbox inside, with a key in the lock. There were record books on the shelf, several sheafs of papers tied with twine, and a glass jar containing small change. In the lockbox was a small packet of greenbacks in a brown wrapper. And two letters.

Winters reached for the letters. Both were addressed in the same hand, to Mr. Harold Chandler, with an address in St. Louis. The date stamped on each envelope was fifteen years old. Winters put them into his pocket.

The record books concerned the store. Franken glanced through them and put them aside. He took the glass jar and the packet of money, saying they belonged to the store also.

Winters thanked him and led the way out to the street. Reb examined the envelopes as they walked to the office. Both were definitely by the same hand, very neat and legible, an office secretary's writing in all probability, the letters all well formed, with no hint of individuality.

In the office they read both letters. They were from the same person, posted about a month apart, a woman who signed herself ''Millie.'' She was in upstate New York and missed Harold terribly but hoped to return to St. Louis soon. She mentioned devotion and love . . . and the pain of separation.

''Love letters!'' Winters said, making a face. ''What the hell are they doing in Kepler's safe?''

Reb stared at the yellowing sheets. ''They weren't sent to him. But if he kept them for fifteen years, they must have some meaning for him.''

''Maybe he was going by that name in St. Louis—what is it, Harold Chandler . . . ?''

''Why did Kepler have only two letters? If it was a love affair, there should be more.'' He frowned at the two envelopes. ''Wait a minute! The initials are the same—H.C. Harold Chandler and Homer Chartis! Do you suppose these were written to Chartis?''

''Jesus! I think you hit it! A love affair with a girl in the office! It fits.''

Reb's mouth turned down. ''So was Chandler his real name?''

Winters grinned. ''I'll write to St. Louie again. Now we getting somewhere.''

''Why did Kepler have the letters? Did he steal them?''

''To blackmail Chartis? Izzat how he got his job here?''

Reb bit his lip. ''If it was that, then he'd want to keep Chartis alive, wouldn't he?''

''Umm, I'd think so.'' The marshal took off his hat, brushed it carefully, and put it back on again. ''We back where we started?''

''No. We know a lot of things—we just can't put them all together. But it looks like I'm going to Carter again.''

''You wearin' out that road. You pro'ly know ever' rock and tree.''

A quick-moving storm passed over Wakefield the day before the southbound stage arrived, bringing a wind that seemed directly out of the Arctic Circle. But the wind dried the roads, and the stagecoach to Carter had no problems with mud.

In town, Reb put up at the Merchant's Hotel and set about locating someone named Chandler.

According to the sheriff's office and the newspaper, which agreed, there were three families in Carter by that name. The first was a middle-aged couple who had never been east of Dyer—which was a few hundred miles in that direction. The second was a widow woman, living with a grown son, whose husband had been a railroad man. His name, she said, had been Frank. The third was a man living alone who did not want to talk to Reb.

"Why not?" Reb asked reasonably.

"What'ave you got to sell?"

"Nothing at all." The man tried to slam the door, but Reb's boot kept it partly open. He could see a thin face and white hair. The man was in his late sixties or seventies.

He yelled, "Get your damned boot outta my door!"

"I've come a long way to talk to you," Reb said. "You may as well let me in."

The man noted the pistol on Reb's hip. "Or you'll shoot me?"

Reb grinned at him. "After I talk to you. Is your name Willis Chandler?"

"What you want wi' me?"

"Let me in and let's talk."

The other hesitated, then stepped back reluctantly, and Reb entered a very neat parlor. It was spacious, with good furniture and landscapes on the walls. The carpet on the floor was bright, and there was even an upright piano against a far wall. It was not the home of a sharecropper.

"You *are* Willis Chandler?"

The man nodded glumly. "What do you want?"

"Your brother was Harold Chandler?"

"Yes . . . but he called himself Homer Chartis out here."

"Then you know about his murder."

"Yes, I read about it. I'm not surprised."

"What d'you mean?"

Chandler made a face "Harold was a miserable man to get along with. He made enemies everywhere—even as a boy he was always in trouble, always fighting. So one of his enemies shot him, that's all. Why should I be surprised?" He backed up to the wide brick fireplace. "I suppose you're the law? I had nothing to do with it."

"I'm not the law. But I want to find out who killed your brother and Mr. Aiken, his store manager."

"You're not the law—then you're a bounty hunter?"

"Yes. It's honest work."

"I don't have to talk to you."

"Yes, that's true, but consider this. Somebody shot your brother and we don't know who or why. But if we don't get him, he could come after you."

Chandler had obviously not thought about that—it showed on his face. He blinked and rubbed his smooth chin nervously. Then he sighed deeply. "What's your name?"

"Wiley. My friends call me Reb."

Chandler frowned. "Haven't I heard or read that name?"

"There have been mentions in various papers," Reb admitted. "I'm surprised to find you living here in Carter."

"I was in business here for many years, ten years before Harold came to Wakefield."

"What kind of business?"

"Selling. I was regional rep for a Kansas City firm. We sold ready-to-wear, household items and the like. I had six crews working for me. Each one had his area. I had a warehouse here in Carter with offices. It was a thriving business—till I finally sold out and retired. That was more than five years ago. I was in business here about twenty years in all, after being in business in Kansas City first."

"So in a way, you were in competition with your brother."

Chandler scowled. "I will always believe that Harold picked Wakefield deliberately to settle and open his huge store. I am convinced he wanted to drive me to the wall." Chandler smiled. "But he couldn't do it. I had the customers and the regular routes. I took goods to the customer's door for only pennies more than it cost them to drive into town and trade with him."

"So you really were enemies."

"In a business sense, yes. My people went where Harold couldn't reach. There's plenty of trade for everyone, and growing. I hated to sell out, but I'm getting on. I take it easy now. . . ."

"How did you two get started?"

"Our father left us a goodly amount, divided between us. He also provided us good solid horse sense. It's too bad he couldn't have pounded some decency into Harold."

"What about Harold's partner in St. Louis? Do you know his name?"

"Yes. I know the name, though I never met the man. It is or was Redfern. They called the store Chandler and Redfern. I don't know what happened to him."

"Can you tell me, when was the last time you saw your brother?"

"It was in St. Louis, a very long time ago. We met by chance in a restaurant. I don't think we exchanged ten words. I remember I left for Kansas City the next day."

"And you never corresponded?"

"Never. I had nothing to say to him."

"How about Harold's enemies? You say you're sure he had plenty of them."

Chandler's mouth turned down. "I know none of them. I only say he was the kind of man to make dozens."

Reb paused. "Here is an important question—do you know why he changed his name?"

"No, I do not." Chandler shook his head. "I was astonished when I heard he had. One of my crew told me he changed it in Vetter. Is that true?"

"I think so. Did you ever know a man named Ben Kepler?"

"No—should I?"

Reb shrugged. "He worked for your brother as a stock clerk. Shortly after we started this investigation, he disappeared. Did you know Harold's first wife?"

"Yes, I did. I thought Harold treated her badly. She was a fine woman. After they parted, I lost track of her. . . ."

"Her name was Mary?"

Chandler was surprised. "Yes! You know more than you tell, don't you! Her name was Mary Addison. She came from West Virginia . . . she may have gone back there."

"But you never met Klara?"

"His second wife? No. I read her name in the papers."

"She inherits the entire estate. You're not in the will. Does that bother you?"

Chandler's voice turned hard. "I don't need or want his money. We never exchanged so much as a penny while he was alive. I'll not start now."

Reb got up to go. "You've been a great help, Mr. Chandler." He smiled. "I won't shoot you after all."

"Thanks." Chandler laughed and put out his hand. "Good luck with the rest of the investigation."

16

The little green cards that were circulating around town were a definite source of worry to Reb . . . in that some drunk might try to back-shoot him to collect the kitty. There were unstable people everywhere, and when one of those was liquored up, who could tell what might happen?

Most treated the cards as lawyer Lisser did, as an excuse to make a bet—winner take all. The kitty was held by the owner of the Red Dog Saloon, its amount posted several times a day for all to read. The last time Reb looked, it was over one hundred forty dollars. A fortune to a drifter. Damn few jaspers could boast of owning one hundred dollars in cash money.

When sober, Jonas Happ was mild and self-effacing. He was not the brightest at the best of times, and when drunk, he was muddled and confused.

He had been sopping up liquor for several hours when Reb entered the saloon for a beer on his way back to the hotel in the early evening. Jonas saw him and wrinkled his low forehead, thinking hard. This was *the* man! It was his only correct conclusion that afternoon.

Jonas was a smallholder with a few acres five or six miles out of town. He had always been a quiet drunk, and the bartenders were used to him and let him drink his fill. He came in once a week to slake his terrible thirst and stagger out to his wagon, occasionally with help. His horse knew the way home.

He fished out his green square and stared at it, mumbling

to himself. The card gave him the right to claim the kitty. In his drunken haze it all made sense.

The saloon was not crowded, and Reb noted Jonas at once, saw the green card and guessed the old man might be fuddled enough to do something foolish. He took his beer from the bar and kept an eye on the old man without seeming to. He sat with his back to the wall, as usual, and relaxed, his thoughts on Lorrie Winters.

Where was she thinking of going to school? It had to be in the East, didn't it? There were no teaching schools west of the Mississippi—as far as he knew.

It was pleasant to sit in the dim room, listening to the piano, sipping beer and thinking about her . . . the way she had looked with the hair fluffed about her face. That must have taken hours to do. Would she have done it—just for her father? It was an interesting idea to contemplate.

And it was equally pleasant to focus on some one person, rather than on women in general, even though he knew nothing would come of it. She would go east in a short while, and he'd probably never see her again. She was getting on toward being a spinster—at twenty-two. At that age most girls were married and had at least one baby. Was it strange that Lorrie had never found the man she wanted to wed? Was it because she had been traveling between schools and home for so long?

Or maybe she was very particular. Well, she would go out of his life and he would never know.

His attention shifted to the old man. Jonas was twisting in his chair, mumbling to himself, and then he managed to pull a pistol from under his coat. He got to his feet after several tries, swaying and blinking his puffy eyes. He turned toward Reb and lifted the pistol, and Reb ducked. The first shot went into the ceiling, and dust filtered down as the bartenders yelled. The second shot smashed something at the rear of the room.

Men were shouting, and Reb scuttled toward the shooter. More shots came and a woman screamed. Powder smoke swirled, and Reb threw himself at the old man and wrenched the gun from his hands. He pushed Jonas into a chair.

The room was suddenly quiet except for a woman's sobbing. A man said, "He hit Cora. . . ."

Reb shoved the pistol into his belt. A woman lay on the floor, with men bending over her. One said, "It's her arm, ain't it?"

A bartender growled at them. "Somebody go for the doc, for crissakes!"

Another said, "Wind a towel around that arm—stop the goddamn bleedin'!"

A few were cursing the drunken Jonas. There was nothing Reb could do for the woman; he picked up Jonas by the scruff and half carried him out to the street. He propelled the grumbling, staggering man to the jail. Jim was standing in the doorway.

"Was that shootin' I heard?" He frowned at Jonas. "That's old Jonas Happ. What'd he do?"

"He just shot a saloon girl in the Red Dog. Put him in a cage, will you?"

"Sure . . . Come on, Jonas." Jim lugged the old man into the back, and Reb sat, hearing the iron door slam. Jim came back. "He kill the girl?"

"No. Hit her in the arm. He was shooting at me. He had one of those little green cards, and he evidently thought it gave him a free shot. Where's the marshal?"

"Went home to supper. I expect he'll be back purty soon." Jim sat on the desk. "Old Jonas never made no trouble. He pro'ly won't even know what he did, when he sobers up."

"Here's his gun." Reb handed it over, and Jim put it in a drawer.

"The marshal was talkin' about going to the council about them cards. . . ."

"He was?"

"Yeah, to make 'em illegal. Said he had a change of heart, it not bein' right to put a bounty on a man like that. So ever' drunk or no-good thinks he can try for the kitty."

"Has he seen George Gibbons about it yet?"

"I don't think so."

Reb smiled. "Well, as the party of the first part, I agree it's a fine idea—making them illegal. I don't need holes in my back."

Jim nodded. "You want some coffee? I made some hot."

"Yes, good. Pour me a cup."

There were noises in the street, and Reb went to the window. A group of men was coming toward the jail office.

Jim put the filled cup on the desk. "What's that racket?"

"Visitors, looks like."

Jim opened the door. There were fifteen or twenty men gathered about the front of the office. Jim said, "What is it?"

The mealy light played on hard faces. One of the men said, "We want Jonas, Jim."

"What for?"

"He went and shot Cora. We going to show him some proper respect."

"Is she hurt bad?"

"The doc is lookin' after her. Open up the jail, Jim."

Jim hesitated and they moved closer, menacingly. The tension was very heavy and thick. One of the men in the back said, "We got us some feathers and a bucket of tar."

Another voice remarked, "We twenty to your one, Jim."

Jim said, "Go on home. I can't give him over to you."

There were growls from the crowd, and Jim edged back. "Go on home, all of you. . . ."

"Git out'n the way, Jim."

Reb stepped out where they could see him, and they halted instantly. He said nothing at all, merely stared from face to face, both thumbs hooked in the cartridge belt.

They looked back at him for several moments, then one said, "Ah, hell . . ." The man turned and walked away. Another followed, and another. In a minute they all straggled back along the dark street, muttering.

Jim said softly, "Jesus! You sure made 'em think twice!"

Reb went inside and picked up the coffee cup, sipping it. "They saw the sensible side of it."

Jim laughed. "That's right. They were scared to death of me!"

Marshal Winters had written to the law in St. Louis, and in due time received an answer. A man named Harold Chandler had been in business in that city with a partner, Len Redfern. The establishment had been called Chandler & Redfern. However, fifteen years previous, Chandler had sold out and gone west to Kansas City. Redfern had continued with the store and was still running it with his sons.

Reb read the letter, frowning. "This man Redfern bought out Chartis—I mean Chandler—and is still operating. He sounds like a solid citizen. Maybe he has more to tell us."

Winters groaned. "Another letter?"

"We want to know why Chandler sold out." Reb refolded the letter. "There's probably no way we can find out if Redfern left St. Louis for any extended period. . . ."

Winters was surprised. "You think maybe he came here to Wakefield and shot Chartis?"

"Isn't it possible? Except for Aiken. He didn't know Aiken. At least we're pretty sure he didn't."

Winters blew out his breath. "He didn't shoot Chartis! Not after fifteen years! He bought Chartis out, and that's it. The end."

"Write the letter."

17

Deputy Jim, making the morning rounds, paused by the open door of the stage depot waiting room. Was that John Franken, carrying his bags out to the southbound Concord?

He crossed the room to the side door for a better look. It was Franken all right, watching the handler sling his two bags into the boot and fasten down the canvas.

The store manager was going somewhere, and it looked like it might be permanent. He had plenty of goods in the bags.

Jim rubbed his neck. Of course, the manager had a perfect right to go any damn where he pleased, and did not have to answer to a town deputy about it. He stood by and watched the hostlers finish up and wave to the driver. The stagecoach rattled out of the yard to the road and headed south. Jim walked out to the road, wondering where Franken was headed.

He mentioned it to the marshal when he got back to the office. Both Winters and Reb were astonished.

"Franken left town?"

"Yeah, and I think he went f'good. He had two heavy bags with 'em."

Reb said, "Let's go by the store and find out why."

"Umm." Winters put out his cigar and they walked to the center of town and into the Chartis mercantile store. They were met by clerk Axel Lynch, who smiled at them. "Morning, gents."

Winters wasted no time. "Why did John Franken leave town?"

At once Axle looked uncomfortable, glancing around. "You best see the new boss. He's Mr. Rankin." He pointed toward the back of the store. "They's a sign there that says Office. He's in there."

"A new manager?" Reb asked. "When did that take place?"

"A couple days ago."

Winters's brows rose. "Who's this Rankin?"

Axle's voice lowered. "We heard he's Miz Chartis's son—by a first marriage. I don't think we s'pose to know it."

Winters nodded. "We won't tell nobody you said it. Come on, Reb." He marched back to the office.

Rankin was a slim, bony-looking man with sparse, blondish hair and steel-rimmed glasses. He was probably about thirty, Reb thought. And not particularly happy to see them. He noted the marshal's badge at once and dredged up a tight smile. "What can I do for you, sir?" He looked hard at Reb.

Winters said, "This's my deputy, Mr. Wiley. We come wondering about John Franken. He got on a stage this morning."

"Is that so?"

"Why did he leave here?"

Rankin folded his arms. "That's company business, Mister . . ."

"Winters."

"Mr. Winters. No town laws have been broken."

"I'm glad t'hear it. But we investigating the murders of Mr. Chartis and Mr. Aiken, which shootings took place in this store. We're mighty curious about Mr. Franken's leaving."

"He resigned."

"Wasn't that sudden?" Reb asked. "He seemed perfectly content a week ago."

"Investigation or no," Rankin said in a hard-edged voice, "I don't see that it's necessary for us in the store to consult with you when internal changes are made. They are really none of your business.''

Winters's voice turned just as hard. ''Was Franken fired, Mr. Rankin?''

''As I said, he resigned.''

Reb said quietly, ''And you are now store manager. . . .''

''Yes, I am.''

''You took over John Franken's job?''

''Obviously.'' Rankin's lip curled.

Reb smiled. ''Where did you come from, Mr. Rankin?''

''You people have no right to question me! Or are you about to arrest me for something? What are the charges, Marshal?''

''We ain't going to arrest you,'' Winters said, pretending great patience. ''But we got a powerful curiosity about Franken.''

''Why not question him, then?''

''He left town. D'you know where he went?''

''I'm sorry,'' Rankin said, in a voice that held no sorrow. ''I simply cannot help you. I know nothing of his movements. I did not know he took the stage this morning, until you told me.''

Winters said in a silky voice, ''There's talk that you're Miz Chartis's son. Is that true?''

Rankin glared at them. Finally he took a long breath and nodded. ''My father died when I was very young.'' He turned away. ''That's all I have to say to you gentlemen.''

They paused outside on the street, and Winters found a cigar and sniffed it absently. ''Where the hell's he been for the last fifteen years?''

''Fascinating question.''

The marshal scratched a match on a hitching post. ''And now he's here. . . .'' He lit the cigar.

''We have to assume his mother sent for him.''

''I guess so. So she doesn't figger to sell out?''

Reb nodded. ''It might be that. But she has moods, as lawyer Lisser told us. Now that her husband is gone, she has no real friends in town. She probably considers herself a stranger . . . so she sent for her son. Does that make sense?"

"I think so. I'd pro'ly do the same in her place."

Deputy Jim was in the office when they walked in. He got up from behind the desk and asked Winters, "How long you want us t'feed old Jonas?"

"Turn him loose tonight. He sobered up?"

"Yeah, but he got no money for a fine."

Reb said, "How bad is the girl hurt?"

"Not bad. The bullet didn't break nothing." Jim shrugged lightly and smiled. "She ain't going to work her trade for a spell. . . ."

"Turn 'im loose after dark," Winters said. "See he gits out of town safe with his wagon."

Jim nodded.

Reb went back to the store later in the afternoon, as it began to get dark and drizzle. He sat on a bench out of the wet and waited. The store closed at five o'clock, according to the sign on the door. He wanted to see where Rankin was staying. He watched the two clerks, Axel and Jody, and Tyler Cole, the accountant, leave and hurry off. Then Rankin came out, pulling a poncho over his clothes. He locked the door and walked rapidly away, hunching his narrow shoulders.

It was no trick to follow him to the Chartis home.

When Reb returned to the office, he said to Winters, "He let himself in with a key, so he's her son all right. It may mean that she didn't trust Franken to run the store, so she got someone who was very close to her to do it—since she couldn't manage it herself."

"That's as good an explanation as any, I guess." Winters brushed ashes off his coat. "I'd be innerested in finding out where he's been all these years. Is they any way of doin' that?"

"I doubt it—unless he tells us."

Winters took his hat off. "He ain't going to give us the time of day, not that one."

* * *

The next morning Reb bought two boxes of shells, got a horse from old Jed Urshel, and rode out onto the prairie, some miles from town. He set up rocks for targets and practiced drawing and firing the .44—with either hand.

Undoubtedly, the police in larger cities had access to all sorts of records and information that they, out in the sticks, would never see . . . might never even know about. Marshal Winters, in his official capacity, could write to those police departments till the cows came home, but unless he could pay for clerk research time, his request would be ignored. He had gotten answers from St. Louis, probably because no research had been necessary. If he asked for information about Rankin, that would certainly be another matter. And anyhow, where would he start? Rankin might have lived in Dyer, a few hundred miles away, or he might have been in Maine or San Francisco . . . or a million places in between.

Reb shook his head and mounted the horse for the ride back. Was he any closer to the truth—to finding the murderer—than when he first started? It didn't seem like it. Maybe he was completely out of his depth, incompetent to unravel such a tangle. A long time ago Marshal Winters had confessed he'd had no police training, and of course Reb had to admit that neither had he. He depended on horse sense and observation, with a little luck mixed in.

Target practice was thirsty work, and he stopped at the Red Dog in town for a beer. The saloon was not crowded, but George Gibbons was there, sitting with Tim Feeny, the bank owner, and Dr. Bartlet, the undertaker.

Gibbons smiled at him, and in a little while came to Reb's table. "Mind if I sit down, Reb?"

"By all means . . ."

Gibbons said, "I thought of something—don't know if it's worth a moment of your time—"

"What is it?"

"I remember one day Joe Aiken told me he had worked for several years for a St. Joseph newspaper, the *Clarion*. I believe he said he was business manager."

"Before he met Chartis . . ."

"I am sure of it, yes." Gibbons frowned. "In the back of my mind, I seem to recall something about Ben Kepler—but it eludes me. Maybe because it's unimportant . . ."

"Anything about Kepler interests me."

The older man rose. "Well, if I think of it, I'll tell you at once."

"Thanks, Mr. Gibbons."

Reb finished the beer and walked to the hotel—changed his mind and went back to the jail office. Marshal Winters was engaged with an older woman who was flushed and angry. Someone was stealing her chickens and she wanted the marshal to do something about it. "What'd we elect you for!"

Winters did his best to convince her to hire a young man or two to guard her coops. The town council would not allow him to hire a deputy to do it.

She went away unconvinced and red-faced.

Winters said in disgust, "I guess it's about time f'me to retire. The crime in this burg is settlin' to a lower level ever' year. Purty soon I'll be arrestin' folks for wearing socks that don't match!"

Reb laughed. "Let's hope not." He sat and told Winters what Gibbons had said. "Maybe the *Clarion* editor can tell us something . . . And when you write to him, be sure to mention Ben Kepler's name."

Winters looked at the ceiling. "Jesus!" He let his breath out. "Since I met you, I been writin' more damned letters than any seventeen people in this town ever wrote in their life! Hell, I never wrote my wife more'n one letter before we was married!"

"I'll bet she cherished it."

"Don't be a smart-mouth! You comin' to supper tomorra night?"

Reb looked at the older man in surprise. "Is that an invitation?"

"Lorrie said to ast you. I dunno what she sees in you, but you know how peculiar women is."

Reb said gravely, "I accept with pleasure."

Winters took off his hat and looked at it. "I told her you would."

George Gibbons sent a young boy to track Reb down the next morning. The boy found Reb in the stable, talking with Jed. He said, "Mr. Reb, he got something to tell you, Mr. Gibbons does."

"Thanks. I'll go see him right now."

Gibbons had a black-bound book open on his desk when Reb arrived in the upstairs office.

"Morning, Reb. Did I take you away from anything?"

"No, nothing important."

"I told you there was something nagging at me, so I looked in my diary—in case I had jotted it down. I've been keeping these books for years, and they've stood me in good stead many a time. Took me all evening to find it because it was three years ago." He tapped the open book. "I was wrong. Aiken told me he met Ben Kepler in Leavenworth, not Vetter. Kepler was using his middle name then, Franklin."

Reb said, "His name was Benjamin Franklin Kepler?"

"Yes. That's not unusual. . . ."

"Why did he change?"

Gibbons turned several pages of the book. "He got into trouble—something about a land deal that went sour. That was in Vetter. That's where I got mixed up. Anyway, he knew Aiken was looking for a place to put down roots, and he suggested Wakefield. Aiken told Chartis that Wakefield was ideal. He could be a very big frog in a small puddle."

"And Chartis went for it."

"Yes."

"So Kepler slid out of Vetter and came to Wakefield using his first name." Reb scratched his nose. "Chartis also knew that his brother was in Carter—I talked to him at length. He thinks Chartis settled in Wakefield to drive him out of business . . . and could not. By the way, did you get the impression, at the time, that Kepler was on the run from the law?"

Gibbons closed his eyes and screwed up his face for a

moment. "I can't be sure one way or the other. But it's a possibility."

"Leavenworth," Winters said curiously. "Calling himself Frank Kepler . . ."

"Or Franklin."

Winters sighed. "I can feel another letter comin' on. The goddamn post office is goin' to get rich offen us."

"Did you write to the *Clarion*?"

"I told Lorrie what to write." He paused. "What's syntax?"

"It has to do with the construction of sentences."

"Well, she says mine is terrible." Winters took off his hat and laid it aside. "You raise a kid and teach 'er how to blow her nose and how to dress herself, and purty soon she is tellin' you how to live and talk and write letters. . . ." He sighed deeply. "I goin' to miss her when she goes away to school. . . ."

"First take her over to the photographer's shop and get some pictures."

Winters snapped his fingers. "Damn me! That's a great idee! Why didn't I think of that?"

"Because you're worrying about syntax. Why didn't you ask her what it was?"

Winters frowned. "You think I want her to know I don't know my butt, for crissakes? I been getting by for a passel of years without knowing no damn syntax." He grinned. "Anyhow, it sounds like it might be connected to them soiled doves in the saloons."

"What time tonight?"

"What? Ohhh, about sundown will be fine." Winters put the hat on and yawned. "I think she fixin' chicken."

18

Winters was quite right, it was chicken—in champagne sauce. It was like no other chicken Reb had ever tasted. It had taken her a week to get the champagne from Carter, Lorrie told them, and she was able to get only one bottle; but it was enough. Her recipe, cut from an eastern news sheet, also called for brandy and port wine, and the dish was served with wild rice.

Reb was astonished at what could be done with chicken. He, like most men on the frontier, was used to plain food—called vittles by nearly all—and a little suspicious of anything exotic.

But the meal Lorrie served them was delicious. They exclaimed over it extravagantly. She had obviously gone to great lengths to make the occasion something special, and she had succeeded, as they told her over and over again.

She even had ice cream for dessert.

"I don't eat like this ever' day," Winters told Reb.

"Daddy!" she said. "You're not shrinking like a month-old radish."

"Oh, you feed me good. But this here chicken tonight could make a man run out and howl at the moon."

She stared at him. "What in the world are you talking about?"

Reb said, "He liked it. Can I help with the dishes?"

"I'll just put them in the pan for now. . . ."

He watched her put a kettle on for hot water and feed sticks into the wood stove.

She said, "What about the investigation?"

"We're making slow progress—if any. But we're really no closer to knowing who murdered the two men than we were a month ago."

"It's hard to get information," Winters said. "If we had a telegraph here, it'd make it easier. But we're on the ass end of civil—sorry. We're at the tail end of civilization out here. Everything is harder and takes longer."

Reb said, "We don't even know *why* the two were killed."

Lorrie nodded. "The classic reasons are money, revenge, jealousy, and the like. None of those fits the case?"

"Any one of them may well fit," Reb replied. "But we haven't enough information to know if it does or not. And there's always the possibility that the killer is a stranger and is long gone and we'll never catch him."

"Amen," said Winters, sipping coffee. "Do I get one cigar in the house?"

Lorrie sighed. "Very well, just one. Then we air the house out."

"I'm a man put upon," Winters said to Reb. "Women are trying to change the goddamn world."

"And we will, one of these days," Lorrie said with conviction. "Did you know there are women's organizations demanding the vote?"

"They wanna vote!" Winters almost yelled. "What the hell they want to vote for?"

"Stop swearing. Men vote. Why shouldn't we?"

"I'll swear if I want to. Women don't—they stay home all day—they don't know enough to vote!"

Lorrie smiled. "They don't know enough? What's syntax, Daddy?"

He grinned at her. "It got to do with sentences."

She looked astonished as he laughed.

He got up to get his cigar. "Damn-fool kids think they know ever'thing!"

It was very dark and raining when he went out to the stable. No worries about a sniper tonight—unless the man were almost within reach. Winters loaned him a poncho, and he rode back to the livery as the storm pelted him. Jed was standing in the wide doorway smoking his pipe.

"Cold rain. Figger it'll snow 'bout next month."

Reb put the horse in a stall and pulled off the saddle and bridle. "You want me t'rub 'im down?"

Jed shook his head. "I'll go 'er. I been lollin' around all afternoon." He hooked a lantern to a nail in the stall. "I hear they got a new manager over to the Chartis store. Feller named Rankin."

"Yes . . ." Old Jed heard all the gossip in town.

"He's the same one was in here couple months back."

Reb was surprised. "He was? You saw him here in town?"

Jeb took the pipe out of his mouth. " 'Course he was. I put my hand on the book. Ridin' a fox-gaited horse. Kind of a squinty-faced gent with glasses."

"That's him. How long was he here?"

"I only seen him a day'r two."

"Thanks." Reb hurried to the hotel in the rain. Rankin had been in town several months past—that would be about the time of the two murders. Was he visiting his mother? Or had he been looking the store over? With Chartis out of the way, his fluttery mother would own everything, and he could probably insinuate himself into the business and control it. And hold the purse strings!

A man could become well off that way.

Reb stripped off wet clothes and slid into bed. It was the first clear indication of motive for murder in the case. Had Rankin shot the two men? He had an enormous lot to gain.

Winters said the next morning, "We'll play hell proving anything like that. Old Jed seen him a couple months ago? That ain't enough to pin anything on him. What do you s'pose he was doin' here?"

"It's an interesting question. Was he looking over the lay of the land? How to get in and out of the store without being seen?"

"He could get a key from his mother." Winters put his

feet up on a pulled-out drawer. "It all makes him a good suspect."

"Yeah, he has an excellent motive. The best so far."

"You mean with Chartis gone, he's in charge?"

"In charge of everything, money included. His mother never interfered with the store's operation."

The marshal squinted, looking out at the street. "How did Chartis and this Rankin get along? I expect they knew each other. . . ."

"Only Mrs. Chartis can tell us those things . . . if she will."

Winters sighed. "Is there any sense asking her?"

It was obvious she did not want to talk to him when Reb sent her a note. She made various excuses, and he did not visit the red-brick house again. Time dragged by.

Old Jed Urshel told him that Klara Chartis had once gone for long drives several times a week. He had supplied a driver and had kept her rig in condition. Now it sat in her stable, gathering dust and cobwebs. She hadn't used the buggy since her husband had been buried.

"Far's I know," Jed said, "she don't go nowheres. Stays in that damned house. The grocery kid brings her vittles ever' week. What the hell do women do all day in a house?"

Reb shrugged. "You're asking the wrong one."

But it made him wonder what Lorrie did all day long. He found himself thinking of her often. She had said nothing at all when they'd had supper, when she expected to go away to school. Maybe she didn't know. But *that* thought was always in his mind, coupled with her.

Marshal Winters received a reply from the editor of the St. Joseph *Clarion*. It was brief; yes, Joe Aiken had worked on the paper as business manager. They had been sorry to see him leave. Franklin Kepler had been his assistant. Both men had been well thought of, and the editor hoped neither was in trouble.

"So Ben Kepler worked for Aiken!" Winters said. "How d'you like that?"

Reb frowned. "I wish I knew how it helps us." He took the letter and reread it. "He tells us facts and nothing much else. *Why* did they leave the paper?"

"To go with Chartis to Vetter?"

"Does that make any sense? What could Chartis offer them that was so good?"

"Maybe better jobs."

"It looks to me—if they did—that they swapped one job for another. To go with a man who was a pain in the butt—as everyone tells us."

Reb propped the letter up on the desk and scowled at it as if it were hiding something from him.

Winters said casually, "When did Chartis change his name?"

Reb swung about, eyes round. He snapped his fingers. "Yes! That's the question! It must have been about this time. When—*Why* did he change his name?"

"Well, if my name was Harold, I'd change it, too."

Reb ignored him and began to pace the office. "Why does anyone change his name after using it for years and years? Does a man get tired of his name? I've never heard of such a thing." He pointed his finger at the marshal. "He changes it because it's necessary for something—like evading the law."

"Maybe . . ."

"What other reason? We know he changed it."

Winters took off his hat and frowned at it. "Chartis was running from the law?"

"Why else would he change his name and travel five hundred miles or more? I believe you mentioned space one day."

"Ummm. I did, didn't I?"

Reb went to the door. "I'm going to talk to Trager at the weekly."

Winters nodded and put the hat on.

Nigel Trager looked exactly the same. He wore a different vest over his shirt, with pencils in the pockets; his hair was a tangle, down over his ears, and he gazed at Reb over his specs.

"Hullo, Reb. What can we do for you?"

"You keep a file of past papers?"

"Of course."

"I'm looking for something—probably an event—I don't know what, but it happened fifteen years ago in Leavenworth or maybe St. Joseph."

Trager smiled. "Something—you don't know what or where? How will you know it when you see it?"

"I know how it sounds." Reb shrugged. "But bear with me. I think it was something that made a man leave town and change his name, all in a hurry. Maybe a killing. Do you often pick up shootings or murder from eastern papers?"

"Oh yes, we might—it depends."

"Would it be possible for me to look through your files of fifteen years ago?"

"This has something to do with our two local murders?"

"It might have a great deal to do with them, yes."

"All right, come this way." Trager led him toward the back, into a long, narrow room that smelled stuffy. Newspapers were neatly piled on marked shelves. Trager walked along the tier, selected one pile, and placed the stack of papers on a table.

"Fifteen years ago, you said."

"Yes."

"Please do not cut or tear out anything. Do I have to say that?"

"No . . ."

The editor supplied several sheets of foolscap. "Copy all you want here."

Reb nodded. "I promise."

Nearly all the papers comprised eight pages, and it was necessary to read or skim about half of each edition. The other half was composed of ads or obviously local items, and woodcuts.

By closing time he had found nothing of interest.

He was at it again the next morning, and spent the day

hunched over the table. Trager brought him coffee now and then.

"Nothing so far?"

"I may be chasing a will-o'-the-wisp."

Late in the afternoon he skimmed over an item concerning the death of Millie Tanner of Leavenworth. The police speculated that she was the victim of a robber.

Reb passed over it, and several editions later he paused. What was nagging at him? Had he overlooked something? He went back and scanned the items again, and then noticed the name: Millie. The two letters found in Kepler's safe were written by "Millie" . . . to Chartis. Was this victim the same person?

If so, had Chartis killed her? And made it look like robbery? He was known to have a quick temper. . . .

Maybe Kepler had stolen the letters as a form of blackmail. With them he could prove a connection between Chartis and the dead girl.

That added up, didn't it?

19

It was indeed Millie Tanner who had written the two letters found in the safe. Her name was on the envelopes.

Marshal Winters read the item that Reb had copied from the paper. He agreed. "I bet you a mule that Joe Aiken got Chartis out of town—probably put him on a stage to Vetter."

"And Chartis made it worth his while. At this point Chartis must have had a pile of money."

"Yep. Chartis kills the girl in a fit of rage, or whatever, and Joe Aiken, who is the level-headed one, gets him out of town and tells him to change his handle." Winters looked pleased. "That's one hell of a good theory."

"And I would guess that Chartis is all upset, so Aiken, and maybe Kepler, go along with him to settle him down. I like the part about changing his name. That's been worrying me for weeks. Why did he do it?"

"So Chartis promises Aiken the moon. . . ."

Reb nodded. "And Aiken brings Kepler, his trusted assistant, along, and Kepler gets a chance to steal the two letters. Maybe Chartis didn't even miss them. Kepler keeps them in case he needs them sometime in the future."

Winters took off his hat. "It must have been something like that. We know he had the two letters." He grinned at Reb. "Some bunch, huh?" He hunted down a cigar and sniffed it. "Did Kepler kill both of them?"

"Why would he?"

"Hell, I dunno. I'm astin' you." He scratched a match

and held it under the cigar tip. "Somebody did. And Kepler was part of the combine."

"But someone tried to kill Kepler."

"Yeah," Winters said in a weary voice. He put the hat on again. "I know. There ain't no end to this case. Ever' time I think maybe we got it licked, it comes around and bites our ass."

He thought of various ways to see Lorrie, short of calling at the house unannounced—which he was certain she would resent. But none of his plans worked out. If she shopped in the town, he could not discover when, and he was not about to ask Winters.

Then one day she came into the office, dressed in a riding outfit, and smiled at them. Winters said, "What you up to, honey?"

"There're some Indians camped along the creek. I'd like to go and look at them. I've never seen Indians close up, and—"

"You stay the hell away from them In'ans!" Winters yelled. "Them tribes ain't civilized!"

"Ooooh, Daddy . . ."

He was red-faced. "They dangerous! That's why! You dunno what the hell they going to do, they find a single woman wanderin' around alone!"

"That's right," Reb said quickly. "I'd better go with you."

She smiled instantly. "Oh, would you, Reb? I do want to see how—"

"Dammit! Don't you take her near them damn In'ans!"

"We'll be safe enough," Reb said soothingly. He took a rifle off the rack and levered it. "Nothing's going to happen." He looked at her. "Do you have a horse?"

"Yes, outside."

Winters took off his hat and flung it down. "You fool kids ain't got the sense God give a horn toad!"

"We'll be all right," Reb said, and followed her to the street. The way she looked this morning, he would take her through the Cherokee Nation and dare them to make a move.

She owned a sorrel mare her father had given her several years ago. She was riding sidesaddle and he gave her an arm up. With the rifle on his shoulder, he walked to the livery, and Jed saddled a roan horse for him.

They rode to the river and along the road that led to Dyer. When they could see the tips of the tepees, they left the road and walked the horses across the sod for half a mile. The Indians were camped along the river, five tepees scattered in a meadow, with a small horse herd grazing nearby. A few near-naked children were playing along the riverbank, but stopped to stare at them.

"What tribe are they?" Lorrie asked.

"I don't know. Possibly Pawnee. I don't know much about Indians. There were never anywhere I grew up."

She reined in. "*Are* they dangerous?"

He made a face. "It all depends. Maybe. Maybe not."

She grinned at him. "That sounds like one of my father's answers."

"Well, it's not an easy question. There're too many variables. Are they on the warpath or not—do they think we'll attack them— But I see women and children, so they're probably peaceful, as long as we are."

There were women near several fires, and a half-dozen older men came out to stare at them.

Reb said, "Let's move away from their horses. Have you seen enough?"

"I—I suppose so. . . ."

They turned north to the road, still walking the horses. It had not been that long since the Custer massacre at the Little Big Horn. There was no telling how these people reacted to that event.

She asked, "Why do they camp so near a town?"

"They probably have things to trade. They want tobacco and staples. Indians are not having it easy since the buffalo are gone."

"Why did the government allow that?"

"Stupidity, I suppose. Politicians a thousand miles away don't care what happens to the tribes. Do you remember what

General Sherman is supposed to have said—that a good Indian is a dead Indian. . . ."

He saw her shiver. "That's a terrible thing! Could that have been government policy?"

Reb shrugged. "It might well have been, and that's one of the things that could make them dangerous. We—I mean the whites—have pushed them off their lands, killed off the buffalo, and tried to herd them onto reservations. They're hunters, not farmers—and they don't vote."

"The eastern tribes are all contained. I suppose the western ones will be one day. . . ." She shook her head. "One entire population is settling itself on another. There are more of us than of them."

Reb swept his arm around to the horizon. "The East *is* pushing west fast. But it's impossible for me to imagine that one day this land will be cities and roads like the East."

"The first settlers from Europe didn't think so about New York, but look at it now!" They halted on the road and she gazed around. "There's so much of this land—more than in the East. Do you really think it will all be settled one day?"

"I hope not. But St. Louis used to be the edge of the wilderness. Now it's part of the East." He paused. "When are you going east to school?"

She glanced at him. "In a few months—in the spring. I've signed up at Coulter Ridge College in Ohio."

"And then what will you do afterward?"

She smiled. "When I graduate, I'll have a teaching credential. Then I'll teach."

They walked the horses toward the town in silence. When she graduated . . . That would be three or four years away. An eternity.

It crossed his mind that he might spend the same amount of time in a law school somewhere . . . and when he graduated, practice law. He might—if he had the tuition. If he solved this Chartis-Aiken case, he might have fifteen hundred dollars for that purpose. . . .

He slid down in front of the livery stable. She put out her

hand and he took it. She said, "Thanks for the company. . . ."

He smiled. "Anytime you want to look at Indians, let me know."

"Thanks."

He watched her ride away, then took the roan into the stable with a long sigh. An eternity.

When the dusty stagecoach reached town the next afternoon from Vetter, it deposited Mrs. Addie Kepler and her baggage in the depot yard. She hired a boy to lug it to the hotel and up to her room, after she signed for one at the desk.

She then went to the Chartis store and inquired about her husband, Ben. "I want to see him. Where is he?"

Axel Lynch asked who she was, and when he learned she was Ben's wife, told her Ben had disappeared and no one knew where he was.

"You best go see the marshal."

"He's disappeared? What d'you mean no one knows where he is?"

"Go talk to the marshal," Axel urged. He gave her directions.

She went reluctantly, and Winters was astonished to hear her name. "Where have you been all this time?"

"I've been at home, of course."

"Where is that, your home?"

"In Loving's Station. That's outside of Kansas City."

"Why did you come here?" Reb asked.

"Because my husband stopped writing and sending me money. We agreed he would send me money every month."

Winters was surprised. "Your husband? You're still married? It's been years and years!"

She lifted her chin. "I don't believe in divorce, sir. Ben wanted his freedom, but he promised—well, he kept his promise for all those years, yes. Where is he?"

Winters explained how Ben had disappeared, leaving out Reb's chase. No one knew exactly where he had gone or why.

There were many unexplained things about the two killings, Chartis and Aiken.

She knew the name Chartis, but had never met him. She made it clear she did not like what she knew of him. She blamed him for many of the things that had come between her and Ben. She knew that Ben worked for Chartis in Wakefield, and she had met Joe Aiken and knew that Ben had worked for him on the St. Joseph paper.

Reb asked, "How did you meet Ben?"

"I met him long before he went with them others. Ben was keeping the books of a Wild West show, and he used to sneak me in to see the performances when the show was in town—that was in Leavenworth. Then the show went broke and Ben got another job in Leavenworth, where we were married. He called himself Frank then. But I always liked Ben better."

"What did Ben tell you about Chartis?"

"Only that he worked for him in Wakefield. I don't think he liked him, but he and Joe Aiken were good friends."

"So that when Aiken went to work for the St. Joseph newspaper, Ben went along?"

"Yes. It paid better, and Ben liked the work."

Reb asked, "Why did you and Ben separate?"

She sighed deeply. "Ben never was a religious man. He never went to church with me. We had many arguments about it. And also I wanted Ben to settle down in one place, but he kept us moving about. Before we were married, he was here, there, and everywhere with the Wild West show—he didn't mind traveling. I thought when we married he would settle down, but he didn't. As soon as Mr. Aiken wanted him to go to St. Joseph, Ben packed up and we went."

"For a year or so . . ."

"Yes. But as soon as Mr. Chartis came along and started talking about moving farther west, Ben was all for it. We had a big fight, and I went back home where my mother lived. I told Ben he had a home there whenever he wanted, but he only sent me money each month."

"Your mother is no longer living?" Reb asked.

"She died four years ago. The property is mine now, but if Ben doesn't send me the money he promised, I'll have to sell it."

Reb said, "So Ben does know about Loving's Station, and where you live?"

"He's never been there, but he knows exactly. Anyhow, he can ask anyone. It's a tiny place and everyone knows me."

20

When Addie Kepler had gone back to the hotel, Winters said, "Ben could be on his way to Loving's Station, huh?"

Reb agreed. "It's one place he might think we'd never find. Of course, if he does go there, half the town will tell him that Mrs. Kepler has gone to Wakefield. So he'll get out fast."

"I suppose so." Winters took off his hat and scratched his gray head. "And then he'll keep goin' east, and that's that—for him."

"Except for one thing."

Winters looked around. "What?"

"Remember Jake Reiss? He was held up out on the grass for supplies and money by someone who resembles Ben Kepler."

Winters groaned. "You're goin' to say Kepler is hanging around town."

"Maybe."

"What for?"

"I dunno what for. But it's very possible he is." Reb squinted at the street. "That means you have to make the rounds—"

"What?"

"—and find out if people—merchants—are missing things a saddle tramp could use."

"*I* have to?"

"You're the marshal, not me. We need to find out especially if food is missing. We want to know anything not reported.''

''People pilfer goods, you know.''

''Yes, but if it's on a regular basis, it's suspicious. I'm wondering if someone like Ben Kepler is stealing food.''

Winters groaned aloud. ''Dammit! First Lorrie, now you!''

''I realize you're put upon, but this happens to be a job that you can do better than anyone else. You've got the badge and the authority.''

''Stop butterin' me up, dammit!'' Winters sighed and got to his feet slowly. He put the hat on, glared at Reb, and went out to the street.

He was gone less than an hour. When he came back to the office, he was grinning. ''Damn if we didn't turn up something!''

''Tell me.''

''I went over to talk to Sam at the general store. He been losin' things. Lost half a crate of airtights a week ago—forgot to take 'em in for the night, along with a sack of spuds. Says some other vittles turned up missing too. He bought a wagonload of corn and turnips and put the shebang in a shed behint the store, and it was broke into.'' He took off his hat and dropped into his chair. ''Talked to Ollie at the hardware store, and he lost some tools. He left 'em back of the store, and they was gone in the morning. That was two days ago.''

''Why don't they report those things?''

Winters sighed. ''They figgered some drifter took 'em—or some of them In'ans over by the river. If so, they gone forever.''

''What kind of tools?''

''Mostly a hatchet.''

Reb nodded, making a face. ''You could build a town with a hatchet.'' He went to the door and gazed out at the empty street. ''I wonder if it was Kepler. . . .''

Winters put the hat on. ''I 'spect you want I should sit there behint the stores all night. . . .''

Reb grinned. ''That'd be a good idea.''

The marshal let his breath out. "Jesus!"

"But there is one thing we ought to do."

"What's that?"

"We ought to make sure the weekly prints a notice of Addie Kepler being in town. Maybe Ben will read it and send her a message or something."

"I'll take care of it." Winters patted his pockets for a cigar. "Lorrie is comin' in later, and we going to have some pitchers took. She home now, sewing on a dress to wear."

Reb made a mental note to see the photographer after the session and order a print or two from him. Winters need know nothing about it.

Nigel Trager came into the office later in the afternoon, after Winters had gone to meet his daughter. "Hullo, Reb . . ."

"Well, Mr. Trager." Reb stood. "Trouble?"

"No, no. I remembered something after you left." Trager was wearing a coat, but looked as rumpled and untidy as ever. Reb dusted off a chair for him, and the editor sat. "It took a while to find it. . . ."

Reb said, "Something in the files?"

"Yes. An unusual item, and I wasn't sure I had used it, matter of fact. The item came from Council Bluffs, a town across the Missouri from Omaha. It concerned a murder."

"An unusual murder?"

"Yes, a love triangle. But I recalled it because of one of the names . . . the name of the man accused and convicted of the shooting."

"Ben Kepler?"

Trager smiled. "No—Howard Rankin, Klara Chartis's son by a previous marriage."

Reb whistled. "When did this shooting take place?"

"More than ten years ago. Rankin has been in jail all those years."

"In jail!" Winters said, astonished. "So that's where he's been!"

"And in the calaboose for a shooting very much like the Chartis-Aiken affair . . . except there was no woman involved, that we know about."

Winters puffed his cigar. "And according to old Jed, Rankin was here in town about the time of the two murders."

"But why would he shoot Chartis?"

Winters frowned and scratched a match, to study the flame. He blew it out after a moment. "Because he saw a chance to take over the store . . . like you said?"

"A murder for money?"

"A damn good motive."

"Umm." Reb rubbed his chin. "What about Aiken? Why him?"

Winter took his hat off. "Because Aiken saw him shoot Chartis?"

"You think Rankin waited two days before shooting Aiken? If Aiken saw him do it, would he wait around? Would he sit in his office with the door open behind him?"

Winters growled. "This goddamn guessin' game ain't going to hold up in court. D'you really figger Rankin shot them two?"

Reb shrugged lightly. "All we have is speculation—and some motivation. Rankin *was* convicted once for shooting someone. That's an inclination."

"Inclination?"

"I mean he was willing to shoot them—so maybe now . . ."

Winters said, "But the reasons are different."

"Yes," Reb admitted. "The first over a girl, and this one over money—if he did it. But I think a good case could be made that he solved his problems with a gun—if he did it."

"Well, whatever. It leaves us high'n dry. We ain't got enough for an arrest or a conviction." He puffed the cigar. "What we need is a signed confession."

Reb laughed. "I've never seen one. Have you?"

"Once—maybe twenny year ago. But the judge throwed it out."

"Why?"

"Because the horse thief didn't write it hisself. Somebody

wrote it for him and he signed it with a X. The judge said he wouldn't allow it. So the horse thief went free—till some ranchers caught up with him. They believed the confession, X and all."

"And they hanged him?"

"Of course. How else you going to teach 'im a lesson?"

That evening before dark, Reb stopped in at the Red Dog for a quiet beer and met Axel Lynch there. Axel was dissatisfied and grumpy. He had been looking around for another job, he told Reb, but had not found one that paid the same as the Chartis store. Most small businessmen could not afford clerks. They hired boys to do chores and deliveries.

The new manager, Rankin, did not know his ass, Axel said. "He don't know a tent peg from a screwdriver, and he can't keep 'is papers straight, not like Joe Aiken did. Even when me and Jody tells him we's out of something, he don't order it."

Reb made sympathetic sounds.

"And he won't lissen! He says, they don't buy here, where they goin' to go?"

Reb nodded. "It *is* the largest store in the territory."

"But they's travelin' hucksters to buy from. I see 'em come through town now'n then." He sipped beer moodily. "I been wonderin' if I could work for one of them."

"It means a lot of sleeping in a wagon. . . ."

Axel nodded gloomily. "I been thinkin' of going back to Kansas City. . . ." He glanced around. "Miz Chartis, she been coming around to the store again, too, these days. See her about once a week. She'n Rankin shut the door and talk in the office." He grinned suddenly. "Talk—they yell at each other."

"They do?"

"They sure as hell do! We can't hear no words, but they make a racket! And when she comes out and sees us, she hides her face in a handkerchief, and it looks like she cryin' out to her buggy."

"They don't get along. . . ."

"No they don't. But she keeps comin' back. Me'n Jody, we think they spattin' about how Rankin runs the store. He's a hardheaded sonofabitch, Rankin is."

"She comes to the store in a buggy?"

"Yep. I think she goin' for drives again like she used to."

Reb was mildly surprised. Klara had said she was afraid to go out. Well, people got over their fears, and grief shouldn't last forever. . . .

He asked Jed about it, and the liveryman confirmed Axel's statement. "Yeah, she taken her rides again. But she don't go outside of town, though. She hires one o'my boys to drive her—just to take the air, she says."

"Does anyone ever go with her?"

"Nope. And she fussy as hell, the boy says. Can't make up her mind about nothing—where she wants to go, what she wants t'do. She's a damn scatterbrained woman."

Reb turned to go and paused. "By the way, does anyone else go for those rides—to take the air?"

"Oh sure. Mr. Gibbons does. He been doing it for quite a spell. Sometimes he takes a scattergun and brings back some birds. He's a good shot."

"He goes alone?"

"Yep. Mostly. Don't r'member when he had somebody along."

"Anyone else?"

"Yeah, Doc Bartlet. He goes out now'n then. Says he got to shake the town dust offen his boots." Jed grinned. "Don't blame him none t'get away from that undertakin' job. Myself, I don't see how a feller could take it up in the first damn place."

"Everyone to his own," Reb said piously.

Jed nodded. "Amen to that."

Bob Bassett, his hand healed, was transferred from the main prison in Albersville to a work gang in the hills. A post road was needed, to cut the distance from one town to another, and guides and planners had finally decided on a route that would require the fewest bridges and cuts where dynamite men would have to be hired.

The hundred or more prisoners were housed in two rows of wooden-floored tents inside a tangled barbed-wire enclosure with a tower where heavily armed guards watched everything that moved.

Each day guards on horseback took the work crews in wagons to the site and assigned them. The guards were always in pairs. No prisoner had yet escaped from any of the gangs. Two had been killed trying.

Each night in the darkened tents the men whispered and discussed plans for escape. One of the loom-large problems was distance and location. None of the men knew exactly where they were. They knew they were a long way from the nearest town, and they could be sure the town was too far for them to reach it on foot. For one thing, they could not save up food for the journey. They were given a meager ration each day, barely enough to maintain strength.

An escapee had to have a horse. Which meant he had to get one from an armed guard. Probably the next thing to impossible. All the guards were experienced men, and they watched each other.

The prisoners whispered about creating diversions—taking the guards' attentions from several daring souls while they pulled another guard off his horse. That plan had one major flaw. While one man might get away, all those who helped would be severely punished. Punishment meant being broken on the wheel. Men died that way or were crippled for life. Was it worth it?

Many plans were discussed, but none was without flaws. Listening to all of them, Bassett was more and more convinced he would serve out his ten-year sentence.

Until the brushfire flared up one night.

All around the camp was thick brush that was mostly dry—it had not rained in two weeks. Bassett woke very late, hearing yells and shouts. He slid out of bed, pulling on pants and boots. All around him men were babbling, getting up and running about in excitement. What the hell had happened? No one knew.

Hurrying outside the tent, Bassett stared at the wall of orange flame that seethed and roared, threatening to engulf the camp. Guards on foot fired shots, ordering the men back into the tents. He saw horses pulling away from the picket lines—and one ran toward him.

Bassett swung aboard—almost without thinking—and dug in his heels, grabbing the hackamore. He headed for the gate at an all-out run, making himself as small a target as he could. Away from the fire it was dark and a dozen horses were running in fright.

He almost ran down the lone guard at the gate. The man scuttled out of the path of the galloping horse and fired half a dozen shots after it. None came close.

He was away in the night, on a fast horse! But without anything but the clothes on his back.

For miles he followed the two-track wagon road, until it began to get light. The gate guard would report that a man had escaped, and the morning count would turn him up missing. A search would be made, but it was a vast, empty land. If he could withstand hunger and the cold, he might have a chance.

Most of all he was determined to return to Wakefield and get even with the man who had shot him—Reb Wiley.

21

Reb met her by chance as she came out of the millinery shop shortly before midday. She halted in surprise. "Reb!"

"Good morning . . ." He stepped up to the boardwalk with a smile. Lorrie was wearing a powder-blue housedress with a tiny flat bustle, white neckline and cuffs. She looked starched and crisp, with a pert little blue hat. She carried a parasol and a small package. She was a feast for the eyes.

It was a cool day, but the sun was peeping out from behind a scattering of milk white clouds and gradually warming the land. He said, "I heard you had your picture taken."

"Yes, Daddy and I did, and I'm eager to see the results." They fell into step, strolling toward the livery. She was apparently on her way home. "It's the first time I've had any taken since I was a little girl."

"I've never had any taken," Reb said. He had never thought of it before, for himself.

"It's an amazing process, photography," she said. "I find it hard to imagine that you can point a little box at someone and have a picture of them come out. But it does . . . well, not right away, but in a few days. I wonder that anyone even thought of doing it."

"I've heard it said we're living in an age of invention . . . though I don't see many hereabouts." He glanced along the empty, dusty street.

She smiled. "I wish someone would invent something better than smelly coal-oil lamps, then. I've been cleaning them all morning."

"I suppose they will, one day. . . ."

She looked at him curiously. "Do you still think you can solve those terrible murders?"

"Why do you say that?"

She sighed lightly. "I think Daddy has given up on them. He seems to believe it's a foolish chase." She bit her lip. "I suppose I shouldn't say that—he'll deny it, I'm sure."

Reb nodded. "I've got too much time and effort invested in the case. I'll have to stick with it awhile longer . . . though I admit it's not going well at the moment."

They walked a bit in silence, then she said, "Are you going to stay a bounty hunter?"

It was the last question he expected. He smiled at her in surprise. "For the time being. It's a living . . . barely."

"It's dangerous!"

He shrugged. "There's that . . . I have thought of studying law. Maybe I will, one day."

She almost clapped her hands. "That's a fine idea, Reb! I'm sure you'd be a success!"

He left her at the livery and watched her stride away. If he were a lawyer, he could stay in one place, in one town perhaps, and maybe even marry a girl like Lorrie. Such things were possible.

Sighing, he went into the stable, got a roan horse from old Jed, and rode out on the road to Hamelin. The buffalo grass was brown, and a few tumbleweeds stirred up the dust of the road. He spent half a day looking and poking, and found no one and no recent tracks. If Ben Kepler had holed up nearby, he had probably moved on anyway, after Deputy Jim and the posse had chased him.

In late afternoon he turned back and made a swing close to the Indian tepees. They were taking them down, preparing to move on. Probably they had a place to go to settle down for the coming winter. Half a dozen dogs came barking after him, and he spurred to leave them behind.

Bob Bassett left the prison road when he reached the open prairie. He got down and covered his tracks with a broom of leaves and twigs, hoping the guards had no tracker and no luck. The odds, he thought, were probably on his side; they would have no idea where he'd gone after he left the work site. How many men could they spare to search for him?

But he had nothing, only a shirt, jeans, and boots. Not even a hat. Not a saddle, a penny, or weapon. And he had only the vaguest idea where he was . . . possibly east of Wakefield. He would have to find a habitation of some kind to get directions and food.

He'd have to beg or steal food.

Then, hours later, he saw the lights—only a few glimmering lantern lights in the far misty distance. He came first on the wide, deeply rutted cattle trail, and followed it to the town.

It was a dark, moonless night, with owls hooting in the trees as he tied the horse at the edge of the place and walked in slowly, peering about him. The town wasn't much, a few saloons, a gen'l store, a blacksmith shop, and little else but near-empty corrals. It was a wide place in the trail called Osage, according to the sign that gave its population: 526.

He was hungry as a starved wolf.

Everything was closed up but one saloon. He glanced in, over the bat wings. Two customers and a bartender, all huddled over the bar, gabbing.

He walked around the row of buildings, and as he expected, the proprietors lived either above or behind their businesses. Those windows were all dark, too. He would certainly make one hell of a lot of noise climbing in, and breaking a window to do it. Not a good idea. All those gents had shooting irons.

He went back to the saloon. A half hour passed before the two customers came out, climbed aboard waiting horses, and disappeared in the night.

Bassett slipped under the bat-wing doors into the saloon without being seen. There was a lonely bottle sitting on a nearby table, and he grabbed it, ducking down as the bartender came around the bar, removing his apron, heading for the front to close the heavy doors for the night.

When the unsuspecting man went by, Bassett rose and hit him a hard blow, catching the other as he fell. Then he closed and locked the doors and ran behind the bar. The till box was not full, but it held a wad of greenbacks and coins. He pocketed all of it.

The man he had hit was probably the saloon owner, and his living quarters were through a back door. Bassett entered with a lantern; he was in a single room that contained a table, one chair, a narrow bed, another lantern, a black stove, and a wire on which clothes hung. There was also a door to the outside, probably leading to a privy; it was well barred.

Over the stove was a shelf with a dozen or more tins of food.

Bassett smiled. Exactly what he needed. He piled half the cans into a sack, with a knife and spoon. Then he pawed through the clothes and found a coat that fit tolerably well, and a poncho. Behind the clothes was a nail in the wall, and hanging from it, a pistol fully loaded. It was a .45 Colt, and he shoved it into his belt happily. Things were going his way!

He pulled the poncho over his head and unbarred the side door into blackness. He had to feel his way past the privy and around the building, gaining the street several doors away from the saloon.

Sliding up onto the horse, he saw no one, and rode west and north. He ate cold beans as he rode, wishing he had stolen a saddle. Bareback was damned uncomfortable.

It rained lightly toward morning and he was glad of the poncho. His beard was growing out, too. He had no razor and hadn't thought to look for one in the saloon. But maybe it was a good idea to let it grow, as a disguise. He'd been clean-shaven the last time he'd been in Wakefield.

So Reb Wiley might not recognize him.

At the trial's end he had yelled he'd get the banker, Feeny. But he cared nothing for him. The man he wanted was Wiley, the man who had shot him. He patted the pistol in his belt, dreaming about how he would plug Wiley. He shot him a hundred times that night.

* * *

A letter came from St. Louis addressed to Marshal Winters. The return address was printed: REDFERN & CO. It was signed by Lenny Redfern and was very short and to the point. Redfern had not seen or heard from Chandler since he had bought the other out.

He added a bit of news, saying that Chandler was evidently a fugitive, a suspect in the shooting death of Millie Tanner. Chandler had been closest to Millie and was known to possess a terrible temper.

Winters handed the letter to Reb, who read it, frowning. "It pretty much confirms what we already knew or suspected."

"Yes." Winters took off his hat. "Is it possible that this Millie person had a brother—or someone else—who came after Chandler-Chartis?"

"That's a long-shot idea!"

"Long shots pay off now and then."

"But nobody's mentioned a brother, or any other relative."

Winters made a long face. "Then I guess we can pin it on Chartis . . . Millie's death, I mean. There's no way he can protest. I say he killed the girl—accident or not—and got the hell out and changed his name because of it."

Reb nodded. "I'll go along with that."

Winters put the hat on. "We'll solve this thing yet."

The next day Marshal Winters received official notice that the county commissioners had authorized the payment of one thousand dollars as a reward for information leading to the arrest and conviction of the killer or killers of Homer Chartis and Joseph Aiken.

Winters walked down the street and handed over the information to Nigel Trager, to be published in the next edition of the paper, due out in two days.

When the paper was distributed, Mrs. Homer Chartis withdrew her offer of fifteen hundred dollars' reward. She gave no reason.

"You figger she knows something?" Winters asked. "Like maybe her son is guilty?"

"If we pin it on Rankin, I can understand why he shot Chartis—for gain. But why did he shoot Aiken?"

"Something we don't know." Winters put his feet up and stared at the street. "We keep comin' back to that. There's a good reason for one to be shot, but not the other."

"Yes—something we don't know." Reb scratched his jaw. "That is probably the answer. We're missing a chunk of the puzzle."

"Is someone lyin' to us?"

"Very possible." Reb nodded. "But how? The only witness is the killer—so far as we know. And Rankin's got a damn good motive. For one of them."

"And he was here in town at the time."

"But motive isn't proof."

"That's the trouble with law," Winters said. "You got to have proof. We ought t'be able to hang that sombitch on the way he looks."

George Gibbons and the town council decided upon a three-day town fair to usher out the summer. They were almost too late with it, it being fall already, but no one was crass enough to state that argument, and so the vote was all aye. Snow was not expected for another month, according to the almanac. The weather was frolickly, but generally sunny, so the placards and banners went up along the street.

At the end of town a racing oval was scraped out using a four-mule team pulling a heavy log. No fair was complete without racing and shooting. A gallery was set up against an earthen wall for both pistol and rifle shooters, and the town merchants chipped in for prizes. Chartis mercantile donated two hundred dollars, much of which went for band uniforms. And for the grant, the words CHARTIS GEN'L STORE was lettered on the big bass drum.

Several days before the fair was to begin, the band paraded up and down the main street and everyone came out to watch and applaud. A ragtag bunch of small boys and dogs followed the bandsmen, pretending to blow instruments. They held their own impromptu parade when the band broke up and retreated to the Red Rooster for beer and chatter.

News of the fair was sent to all the nearest towns, even to Vetter, and it was hoped they might draw as many as two hundred souls.

With money to spend.

22

The council was delighted when people flocked into town from Hamelin, Carter, one or two from Ganz Siding, and even a handful from far-off Vetter. All in all, many more than two hundred. People were starved for entertainment.

Most of the visitors camped in the fields with their wagons, where they quickly introduced themselves to neighbors. The campsite buzzed like busy hives, and nearly all put the kids to bed early and sat around the fires till long after dark.

The placards in town announced a street dance, to be held the first night of the fair. The street was blocked off and lanterns were strung along it and around the hastily built bandstand. When the big night arrived, people gathered in the street and yelled and whistled as the bandsmen took their places.

Reb left the hotel at dusk and walked slowly along the lighted street. The colored lanterns made the street bright and gave it a very gala appearance; the shadows hid the lack of paint and weather-scarring. He watched as the crowds closed in about the bandstand. The musicians were fussily arranging themselves, tuning their instruments, talking to friends among the spectators.

All the merchants had closed their shops, with the exception of the saloons. They closed only for disasters—and sometimes not even then. George Gibbons came along the walk, with a smile and wave to him, and crossed the street, pushing through the throng to the bandstand.

And then he saw Lorrie.

She was walking toward him, pausing to speak to someone in the crowd now and again. She wore a dark blue dress he'd never seen before. The full skirt brushed her shoetops, and she had a yellow scarf of some silken material about her neck, with her brown hair fluffed the way it had been at the dinner. She looked beautiful.

Three young men followed her, snickering among themselves, obviously eyeing her. They stopped short when Reb stepped into the light of a lantern and spoke to her.

Lorrie glanced around and smiled, holding out her hand to him. "Reb! I'm glad to see you!"

"Me, too. Where's your father?"

"He said he'd be along after a bit. You know how he is. He never hurries to anything."

The musicians began to play, and she stepped down to the street. "You're just in time to ask me to dance."

He was embarrassed. "I—I don't know much about dancing. . . ."

Her brows arched. "You don't? I hardly believe it!"

He stepped down to the street. "It was never a part of my education—such as it is."

"Well, we'll remedy that. It's easy. See, everyone is doing fine."

Most of the men were stomping about with rather more enthusiasm than grace, he thought. Not one seemed worried about how he appeared, and the women were equally eager to whirl about.

"What do I do?" he asked lamely.

She took his right hand and placed it on her waist. "Put this hand here, and hold my other one—yes, that's right. Now step out like the others are doing—keep time to the music."

He did as he was told, enjoying the feel of his hand about her slender waist. It was the first time he had touched her, other than something like shaking hands. He tried to move in time with the music, and she laughed, saying he was a born dancer.

His natural coordination came to his aid, and in moments he was moving as gracefully as she and grinning like a schoolboy. They moved among the crowd, laughing and carefree as children. The musicians played a half-dozen numbers before they took a breather. Everyone shouted and clapped, and Reb saw George Gibbons standing with Marshal Winters on the boardwalk, both of them puffing cigars and looking expansive.

The crowd stood impatiently, in pairs, chattering. Overhead, the stars were very bright as Reb walked with Lorrie, away from the bandstand. Their hands touched, and she grasped his at once, and he looked at her. Her profile told him nothing; she did not squeeze his hand, merely held it.

Then she said, "Do you always wear that gun?'"

"I'm afraid so . . ." He shrugged lightly. "The business I'm in . . ." They paused at the edge of the crowd, and he said, "Your father's been a lawman for many years. Surely you're used to guns."

"Yes. And yes he has been." She sighed. "I used to think it was wonderful, him wearing the star. But now—I guess I realize the danger it could bring."

"Wakefield is a peaceful town. Not at all like some."

She smiled. "He tells me that all the time. And he has a deputy." She looked at the dark sky. "And he is talking more and more about retiring. . . ."

He took her arm. "The music's starting again."

They danced till the musicians paused once more, and this time discovered that some ladies had set up a long table and were serving punch. Reb got two glasses and handed Lorrie one.

She sipped it and looked at him. "There's nothing in it but fruit punch."

He laughed. "Did you think there would be?"

"I'm sure my father had something to do with that."

"Probably."

Bob Bassett approached Wakefield very late in the afternoon. When he could see chimney smoke in the distance, he moved off the road into a small wood and slid down. It would be smart to wait for dark. To ride in on a horse without a saddle would attract attention. People would stare and probably remember him.

He was hungry; the food cans he had stolen were gone, except one can of beans, and he could not stomach another one, cold.

Forcing himself to be patient, he waited till dusk, then walked toward the town, and was astonished when he came near to see the wagons and the dozens of people camping in the fields. He stopped a young boy and learned that the town was holding a fair, starting tomorrow.

That was a bit of luck! Things were definitely going his way! The town would be full of strangers. He could mingle with them and never be noticed . . . as he looked for Reb Wiley.

He had supper in a restaurant, then sat in a chair on the walk, watching the crowds. There must have been a hundred people wandering about. Three or four carpenters were putting finishing touches on a bandstand and hanging red, white, and blue bunting across the front and sides of it.

But he did not see Wiley.

When it got late, he slept in someone's barn on the edge of town, curled in a hayloft. He left at sunup, avoiding the owner, and sat by the restaurant on a bench, waiting till it opened.

As he waited, he thought about how he would center Wiley. He had no real plan. Maybe circumstances would be good enough to arrange themselves favorably, now that his luck was running strong. Of course, the weakness of any plan that called for the ventilation of Wiley was the lack of a rifle. He would have to get close with the pistol.

And he knew Wiley was considered deadly. . . .

But the man did not have eyes in the back of his head.

He did nothing all day but move from one spot to another, following the shade, the day being warm. In the afternoon he walked to the racing oval and watched a dozen races, but did not bet. The shooting gallery provided a constant banging, as if a small war were going on nearby. There were a half-dozen lean-to concessions selling candy and gimcracks, but he ignored them. In town he sat in the Hole Card Saloon for several hours till it began to get dark.

When he heard the band begin to play, he went out and prowled along the boardwalk, watching the grinning dancers.

And then he saw Wiley.

The man wore a buckskin coat with long fringe, and had a red headband—exactly as he remembered. Wiley also wore a walnut-handled revolver partially concealed by the coat. He was dancing with a very pretty girl. . . . He was a big man, moving with a catlike grace, and looked supremely confident.

Bassett stared at his enemy, clenching the hands down at his sides. Was it going to be possible to get close to Wiley's back? He sure as hell would not face him!

The musicians were still playing, though the crowd had thinned by half, when Lorrie begged off, saying she could not dance another step. She leaned against him, and he walked her away from the music. "I'll take you home."

He looked about for Winters but did not see him.

She wanted to rest on a bench, so they sat for a few moments, and he said, "Your father is thinking about retiring?"

"Yes, he is." She rubbed her feet. "I suspect he worries that something might come along that he couldn't handle."

Reb nodded, recalling how Winters had recruited him to work on the Chartis-Aiken murders.

She said, "He and Mr. Gibbons have been talking about going into business together. I don't know how far the talks have gone. . . ."

"Mr. Gibbons owns the hardware store, doesn't he?"

"Yes, I think so."

They walked away from the crowds and the lanterns. Where the light did not reach the street, it was dark and shadowy, and Reb glanced behind them several times. He was mildly surprised that she noticed.

"What're you doing?"

"Habit," he said.

She glanced over her shoulder. "Do you see something?"

"No. Nothing."

She gave a little laugh. "I've never met anyone like you."

"Is that a compliment?"

"I'm not sure what it is." She let her breath out. "I must admit I feel very safe with you, but at the same time I'm constantly aware there might be danger. I mean, danger where you are."

He smiled. "Old habits are hard to lay aside. But I doubt if there's any danger close by tonight."

"Well, I hope not. It would be a shame to spoil a fine evening."

"Yes, it would. . . ."

The house was dark when they approached it and stood on the porch. She said, "Daddy's not here. He's probably in the Red Rooster with his friends. . . ."

"He doesn't worry about you?"

She opened the door. "He knows I'm with you. I saw him watching us." She faced him. "Good night, Reb. I had a wonderful time. . . ."

"There're two more days of the fair."

"Yes, I wouldn't miss them. We probably won't have any more good times till Christmas."

He touched her hand. "Till tomorrow, then. . . ."

She went up on tiptoe suddenly and kissed him. "Good night."

Then she was gone. Reb stood rooted for several moments, staring at the closed door. He had been wondering how he might manage a kiss, but had devised no plan—but she had been certain and direct. She hadn't worried about ploys and plans. He turned away, laughing at himself. This was an experience at which he was a rank amateur. He'd had no truck at all with women like Lorrie, because there were so few respectable women on the frontier—who weren't married.

He walked slowly back to the main street, feeling her kiss. . . . It was a very bold thing for her to do, and it surely meant that a fire was burning somewhere, perhaps not a blazing torch, but a flame nevertheless. He smiled. A tiny flame that might be nurtured? It made him feel a little light-headed.

People were still dancing, though fewer than before. The band sounded tired, and a few minutes after he returned, they played their last tune and began to pack their instruments and shrug into coats.

Reb went into the Red Rooster, where Winters waved to him. He ordered a beer and looked at the slow-ticking Seth Thomas on the wall. It was late; almost nine-thirty.

Bob Bassett sat at the far end of the bar. He stiffened when he saw Reb Wiley come through the bat wings, but he felt secure in his unkempt long hair and the beard. It had been a while since Wiley, or anyone else in this town, had seen him, and then he'd been clean-shaven. He stared at himself in the back-bar mirror and hardly recognized the face that gazed back at him.

To the other men in the room he was probably no more than a poor saddle tramp, passing through. When he'd entered and sat at the bar, the bartender had hesitated before serving him. Bassett had slapped money on the mahogany to prove he could pay.

Without seeming to, he watched his enemy take beer to a table to sit with several others, one of whom he recognized as the town law.

Bassett frowned at the scar in his hand and rubbed it idly. The doc had been right; it was not the same, the hand. It would never be the same. He was slow with a gun now, and had been unable to teach himself to use his left.

And the man sitting there across the room was responsible for it all.

23

Marshal Winters, along with every other peace officer in the territory, received a notice in due time that Bob Bassett had escaped from custody and should be considered dangerous. A five-hundred-dollar reward was offered for him, dead or alive. It was not known where he'd gone or if he'd had help in making his escape from the work camp.

Winters read the notice and passed it to Reb. "He made a threat against Tim Feeny. You figger he'll come here?"

"If we're guessing, I'd guess he might. But owlhoots are like Indians. They're usually unpredictable." Someone was singing in an off-key monotone from the jail area. "You collared some drunks last night?"

"Jim brought in two. It was purty quiet for a town party. No shootin' at all." Winters took off his hat and stretched, yawning. "Seems t'me that Bassett feller would be mostly gunning for you. You're the one shot him."

Reb nodded. "I'm sure he remembers." He studied the notice. "I wish to hell we had a telegraph in town. I'd like to know a lot more about his breakout."

"Yeah. Them work camps is well guarded. He might have a gang with him." Winters brushed off the hat carefully. "This is Saturday and they's a flock of strangers in town. He could be one of 'em. You remember what he looks like?"

"Yes, I certainly do. Broken nose and all."

"Well, watch your back."

* * *

A small spate of trouble erupted in the afternoon. Too many were passing bottles about, and several free souls began shooting at the O's in signboards, or at birds flying over. Deputy Jim and Marshal Winters rounded up a half-dozen and hauled them off to the pokey after disarming them.

But as the day waned, more and more celebrants, fired up on prime squeezin's, began letting off steam with six-guns. Bob Bassett idled along the boardwalk, watching for Reb Wiley, pleased by the noise. One more shot, centered on Wiley, would never be noticed. . . .

Long shadows stretched across the street, and people were straggling in from the fields, mingling with the townsfolk, ready to dance again.

The bandsmen struggled into their red and white uniforms, some of them passing bottles back and forth. Other men, with short ladders, were lighting the colored lanterns along the wide street.

The two lawmen could not be everywhere. They arrested the falling-down drunks, doused a number of staggerers in handy water troughs, but others eluded them and continued to fire into the air as if it were the Fourth of July.

Reb stayed off the main street, heeding the marshal's advice. He circled around by way of the alley behind the stores and came out between two buildings, the photographer's shop and the Hole Card Saloon, nearly opposite the bandstand. When Lorrie came to the dance, she would probably come here first.

It was dusk, but the band had not yet begun to play. They were arranging lanterns and conferring among themselves, possibly discussing what they would play. One man was attaching the kitty box where it could be easily reached by the dancers.

There seemed to be hundreds of people milling in the street, many more than the night before, and all apparently in a holiday mood, a scattering of older children among them.

Hoping Lorrie would come, Reb waited, scanning the faces of the passersby; nearly all were strangers. He did not notice the poorly dressed, scraggly-bearded man who hugged the front of the Hole Card, moving slowly toward him.

Lorrie had gone to her father's office, and finding it locked, came back toward the bandstand. She smiled, seeing Reb in the shadows of the building. He was a few feet from the passing throng, looking off to his right.

And then she saw the bearded man draw his pistol!

The man pulled back the hammer and began to hurry toward Reb, only a dozen feet away.

She screamed, "Reb!"

She saw Reb turn and move at the same time as the bearded man fired, again and again. Both men disappeared from view, into the shadows between the two buildings, and there were more shots.

Lorrie stopped short, her heart pounding. Reb had been gunned down! How could he have survived all those shots? She leaned against the wall, feeling weak. It had happened so suddenly. . . . She watched a crowd of men gathering, muttering, and someone brought a lantern.

Then, to her astonishment, Reb appeared. He was reloading his revolver, talking to the men about him, who rushed into the space with more lanterns. He saw her then and, holstering the gun, went to her.

"Thanks for the warning. . . ." He took her hands. "Are you all right?"

"I—I thought you were dead!"

He pulled her to a bench and they sat. Reb said, "He was excited, yanking the trigger."

"Who was he?"

"I dunno. I didn't get a good look at him. Maybe one of those gents with a green ticket."

"Daddy told me they were all called in."

"Maybe someone didn't get the word." He looked at her keenly. "Are you sure you're—"

"I'm fine. Just let me get my breath."

He got up and went into the space between the buildings where the body lay. The marshal had been sent for, someone told him, and Doc Bartlet was on his way. Several lanterns shone on the face of the victim—the man looked familiar. Reb knelt and turned the head, and the broken nose was evident. Bassett! He lifted the dead man's right hand and nodded at the scar. Bob Bassett, all right!

He glanced around as Marshal Winters said, "Who is he?"

Reb got up. "Bob Bassett. Remember him?"

Winters grunted. "So the sombitch came back. He didn't have the good sense God give a frog. Let's see his gun."

Reb handed it over.

"Five shots fired," Winters said, turning the cylinder. "He hit you?" He peered at Reb, who shook his head.

"He was too eager."

"He was too dumb," Winters corrected, shoving the pistol into his belt. "He's worth five hunnerd, you know."

"Yes."

Winters motioned to the others. "Somebody tell Doc to bring his wagon, and git on out to the street you-all. Tell the band to get to playin'. This here party is over."

They waited till Doc Bartlet loaded the body onto his wagon and drove away. Then they walked back to the jail office. Lorrie was pale and tired-looking. She dropped into a chair, and Winters brought her a glass of water. "You want a little brandy, daughter? You look peaked."

"No—this'll be fine. It's just that I was never close to a shooting before. It sort of takes your breath away."

"That's a fact." Winters motioned to Reb. "What happened?"

Reb shrugged. "Lorrie probably saved my bacon. When she yelled, I dropped flat and his shots went over my head. When he came rushing in—" He shrugged again. "—it was all over." He smiled at her. "He thought he had me cold, but he didn't know about Lorrie."

"Did I yell?" she said. "I don't know what happened—it was all so sudden. It was over in a second or two."

"Gunfights have a way of bein' sudden," Winters said gravely. "You feel all right, daughter? We could take you home."

She smiled at him. "I'm all right now, Daddy." She paused. "I saw that man draw his gun—he was staring at Reb and his mouth was all drawn back over his teeth—he looked like a wolf! Then he started to run at Reb and shoot—and that's when I—" She took a long breath. "That's when I thought Reb was dead." She gulped the rest of the water and handed the glass back. "I'm going—to see that in a nightmare!"

"Put it out of your head, daughter. It all come out good."

Lorrie protested that she felt all right, but when they went back to the street where people were dancing and laughing, she was obviously out of the mood. Reb brought her some punch and they sat on the sidelines, watching the others. One of them was Axel Lynch, dancing with a buxom woman with great enthusiasm. Even Doc Bartlet, the undertaker, was there, sipping from a flask as he stood near the bandstand.

Lorrie said all at once, "How can you live like that?"

"What do you mean?" He gazed at her, brows raised.

"That man, the one who—who was shot. You knew he'd come looking for you, isn't that so?"

"I thought he might."

She glanced at him. "And yet you went on as though nothing would happen. How can you do that?"

He was mildly surprised. What did she expect him to do? He said, "I don't know if I can explain it. I guess it's just part of my job."

"He could have killed you tonight!"

"But he didn't."

She faced him. "And you can sit here calmly and talk about it . . ."

"What else can I do?"

She fell silent. Hands clasped in her lap, she stared at the dancers, then she rose, and Reb got up beside her.

"Would you like to dance?"

"No." She sighed deeply. "I—I want to go home."

He walked with her, and they were silent most of the way. At the front door he said, "I'm sorry about the shooting.

I mean, I'm sorry it had to happen in front of you.'' It sounded very lame.

She looked up at him. ''Yes—but it had to happen, didn't it? Tonight or some other time.''

''I'm afraid so.''

She slid her arms about him in a rush and kissed him hard. Then she was gone and the door closed behind her.

Turning, he walked slowly out to the dark street. He stared at the house for a few moments. Did she want him to change, to become someone else? How could he do that? Of course, she had a completely different view of his life. Probably what seemed reasonable to him was very foreign to her. They stood on different sides of an abyss . . . and there was no bridge. Unless he did somehow change and entered a new kind of life. But he could not—not for the moment, anyhow.

Well, they would talk again. After all, her father was a lawman, and he was hale after years and years. . . .

He returned to the festivities. It was growing late, after ten o'clock, and the dancers were fewer. There was no shooting into the dark sky. Reb went on to the hotel and up to his room. Perhaps tomorrow would bring another circumstance unthought of today. . . .

And it did.

Marshal Winters did not appear in the jail office until late morning. A spate of wanted flyers had come in the mail, and Reb was studying them when Winters walked in looking glum. He took off his hat and slumped in his desk chair.

Reb said, ''What is it?''

A big sigh. ''She's gone.''

''What? Who's gone?''

''Lorrie. She took the stage to the railroad this mornin'. She going to stay with friends in Ohio till school starts.''

24

He rode out onto the prairie, letting the horse take him. Crossing the river at a shallows, he splashed through the muddied drift of it and waded past cattail rushes. She was gone—and so abruptly, leaving a void he had not known he could feel!

The thought of galloping after her had risen at once to his mind—he might easily catch her at Ganz Siding, but if she had gone this way, she did not want to be caught.

A flock of birds lifted and swooped across the brown grass in his path. Others wrangled and chattered in the brush nearby, and he was conscious of a loneliness he had never felt before.

He paused on a rise and looked back at the dark smudge of the town in the distance. Smoke drifted off to the east and became lost in the haze. A few yellow leaves, picked by a spiraling wind, fluttered past and disappeared into the brush as he turned the horse.

She was gone. And probably out of his life forever, with her oblique glances and the several kisses that had made shivers race through his body. He sighed deeply, looking at the mottled sky. She had picked the right day; it was leaden and rain-laden, eager to spill its promise. And far off he saw evidences of the wind coming toward him, rippling the grass and flinging loose soil carelessly into the air.

It began to rain as he reached the town and turned into the livery. Old Jed, with puffy eyes, took the horse. "You jes' barely beat the wet, son."

Refusing the offer of a poncho, Reb trudged to the hotel, perversely enjoying the beat of the rain on his back. He arrived soaking wet and went into the bathhouse to strip off the clothes and wring them out. Then, with a towel about his waist and the cartridge belt and pistol over one shoulder, wet clothes on the other, and carrying his boots, he climbed to the room, ignoring the stares.

He had barely pulled on dry jeans and a shirt when Marshal Winters rapped on the door. He came in, taking off his hat, and looked curiously at the wet clothes hanging over a chair.

"You been out scurryin' around in the rain?"

"I was, yes." Reb sat on the bed and pointed to the other chair. "Did you come to tell me not to?"

"I come to tell you I was talkin' to Axel Lynch. He had a thing to say."

"Oh? What about?"

"Rankin. Axel, he says Rankin been taking some afternoons off, riding out on the grass."

Reb frowned. "Does he know why?"

"I guess not."

"Why did he tell you, then?"

Winters let his breath out as if put upon. "Because we ast him a long time ago to tell us anything different. This was different. He's a cooperative soul, Axel is."

Reb smiled. "And he doesn't like Rankin."

"That's true. But why you figger Rankin is doin' that? Is he meetin' somebody—maybe Ben Kepler?"

"Kepler? How would he even *know* Ben Kepler?"

"Ummm. That's right. Rankin was in jail till a little bit ago."

Reb shrugged. "It may not mean anything, his riding out of town. Maybe he gets restless." He did not mention that he himself had ridden out onto the prairie that very morning.

"Maybe so." Winters put the hat on. "And maybe Axel is wrong." He went to the door and came back. "By the way, Lorrie left you a letter." He took it from an inside pocket and handed it over. "It was propped on the dresser in her room, and I didn't see it till a minute ago."

"Thanks." Reb stared at the envelope, nodding as Winters said good-bye and left. He bit his lip and tore the envelope open. The note was brief:

> Dear Reb:
> At the risk of sounding pedantic, we must all do what we have to do. I often wish it were otherwise. I hope you will study law and hang out your shingle. And perhaps we will meet again in the future, in other circumstances.
>
> Fondly,
> Lorrie

He read it several times, then folded it carefully and put it back into the envelope. That damned Bassett! Why did he have to show up and get himself dead—almost in front of her? It was probably the violence that made her realize the kind of life he led.

Sighing, he stood by the window and looked out at the rain. Maybe they would meet again one day—maybe.

Two nights later Sam Ponder, grocery store owner, shot a prowler behind his store. The sound of the shot brought Deputy Jim, who was on his rounds. He stumbled on the wounded man, and Sam brought a lantern. Together they made a startling discovery. The man on the ground was Ben Kepler!

Kepler had been trying to break into a shed behind the store, obviously in search of food. He was shot in the lungs and was bleeding profusely. Jim bound up the wound as best he could, and Sam went for Doc Bartlet. He examined the wound when he arrived, and declared the victim was in a very bad way and had lost a great deal of blood. A lung shot was terribly serious.

A passel of men were recruited from the Red Rooster, and someone brought a door. Kepler was put on it and they carried him to the jail and laid him on a bunk, for lack of a better place.

Reb stayed in an adjoining cell the rest of the night, unable to sleep because of the hurt man's agony. No one had any laudanum to give him. In the morning Kepler was too weak to talk. His breath was only a whisper and he was sinking fast.

Doc Bartlet looked at him again in the light and shook his head. In the office he said, "There isn't anything I know to do for him. He doesn't have long, poor soul. . . ."

They fed him some broth when he was conscious, but he could not answer questions. His clothes were a sight, worn and ragged. He had been living a hand-to-mouth existence. His horse was found, tied to a post in the alley. Jim led the animal to the livery. In the saddlebags behind the saddle cantle was a revolver and a can of coffee, a small bag of salt, a comb, two spoons, and a block of matches.

"Poor as a goddamn frog," Winters said. "Worse than poor, for a fact. Why the hell's he been hidin' out all this time for?"

"He's got a reason," Reb replied. "If we can get it out of him."

"Yeah, before he kicks off. He's in damn bad shape."

Winters brought in a neighbor woman, Mrs. Skirrow, to care for Kepler as best she could.

She went into the cell and came out. "He smells pretty bad. Where's he been living, in a prairie dog hole?"

"I think so," Winters said. "Hold your nose and tend to him. We want 'im t'answer some questions."

"Poor man, he needs a real doc."

"I know. Keep him alive if you can. I'll send to Carter. Maybe we can get a doc to come up here." Winters lifted his shoulders. "It's all we can do."

Kepler was coughing up blood and had a fever. Mrs. Skirrow managed to sit him up to ease the vomiting and coughing, and even fed him more broth.

Reb asked him why he had run off from town, but he did not answer, giving no sign that he had heard.

Nigel Trager came to the office to ask about him. "Everyone in town knows he's here, Bill. What can you tell me, for the paper?"

"Don't print nothing," Winters said. "He hasn't told us a thing."

"Do you think he knows who did the murders?"

"Please don't speculate," Reb said quickly. "The marshal's right. It's better right now to say nothing."

"Maybe he's guilty himself."

"When we know something," Winters said definitely, "we'll let you know. All right?"

"You're keeping something back, aren't you?"

Winters pointed to the door. "Good-bye, Mr. Trager. We'll see you-all in church."

Reb entered the Chartis store just after midday and looked about for Axel Lynch. The big store was deserted, not a customer in view. It was a cold, rainy day, so perhaps shoppers were staying home.

As he walked toward the rear, Jody Fogle waved to him. Jody was eating his lunch, spread out on a desktop, where he could watch the store entrance.

"Me'n Axel brings our lunch most days," he said. "You wanna see him? He's out back somewheres. You want I should find him f'you?"

"No, finish your lunch. I'm in no hurry."

"Sure. He'll be in directly."

Reb wandered about, looking at the vast selection of goods and articles for sale. There was even a display of blacksmith's tools, and near it several cases of handguns, and more on the wall behind them, revolvers and derringers and a large circle of hunting knives fastened to an imitation buffalo robe.

He examined a Colt, opening the loading gate and spinning the cylinder. One of these days he should retire his old .44 and buy himself a new pistol. . . . He picked a catalog off the glass case and sat down on a chair in a corner to turn the pages.

A woman came along the aisle and stopped in front of the revolver case, and Reb was surprised to see it was Klara

Chartis. She wore a dark blue coat over a pale blue dress that brushed her black shoes. She was bareheaded and had a dark red scarf about her neck. She did not notice him in the corner.

He saw her smile and pick up a single-action Peacemaker. She drew back the hammer and let it down, then with a quick movement deftly twirled the gun by the trigger guard, laid it gently on the case, and went on to the back.

Reb stared after her in astonishment. What he had just seen took hours and hours of diligent practice! *That* was the helpless, fluttery female Marshal Winters talked about!

He got up and went out to the street. The rain had let up. There was a covered buggy standing in front of the door, with a single horse in the shafts. He moved along the walk, hearing voices behind him. Mrs. Chartis and her son, Rankin, came out of the store and got into the buggy. Reb watched them drive out of town toward the south.

He hurried to the jail office to tell Marshal Winters what he had just seen, but Winters was not there. Mrs. Skirrow did not know where he had gone.

But she had other news. "He's talked some, Mr. Kepler has. I'm pretty sure he knows he's dyin'."

Reb asked, "He talked to you?"

"Yes." She nodded, clasping her hands in front of her apron. She did not look at him. "He told me . . ." She paused and took a breath. "He told me—that he shot Mr. Aiken!"

Reb paced the room and came back to stand in front of her. "He said that, you're sure?"

"Yes. Like I told you, he knows he's dyin'—him coughin' up all that blood like he does. An' he's weak and he hurts. . . ."

"What else did he say?"

She frowned, biting her lower lip. "He's hard to understand. He said he shot Joe Aiken because they quarreled over Miz Chartis—a terrible fight. He said she left him and went to Aiken."

Reb was astonished. "A lovers' quarrel?"

She nodded quickly. "And her a married woman!"

"What about Chartis?" he demanded. "Did he shoot him, too?"

"I asked him that, and he said no. He said Klara did it. That's why he left. He was afraid of her." Mrs. Skirrow rubbed her hands together. "I best get back in there. . . ."

Reb nodded absently, looking out at the street. *Had* Klara Chartis shot her husband? Was it possible that she and Ben Kepler had had an affair for years—and then she had become involved with the handsome Joe Aiken? Maybe she and Aiken planned to get rid of Chartis—and then Ben Kepler had wrecked the plans. Why wasn't it possible? It was! It was very damned likely!

He went looking for Winters and found him in the Red Rooster, waiting to talk to George Gibbons. Reb took him aside; they sat at a table by the wall, waving off the barman. Reb related what Mrs. Skirrow had told him, finishing with what he had seen in the Chartis store.

Winters was astounded. "Is that the goddam truth?"

"She handled that gun as good as me."

"I'm damned!"

"Miz Skirrow says she is certain Ben Kepler knows he is dying. Does a dying man lie?"

Winters let his breath out slowly. "I guess not. It'd make a hell of a bad impression at the Pearly Gates. So—they's two murderers instead of one."

"Yes. That's why nothing fitted. We had motives for one, but not both. I'm certain now that Klara Chartis knew that Ben had shot Joe Aiken, so she shot her husband, Chartis, to blame it on him, too. She wanted to get rid of Chartis anyway. And with him dead, she is rich and Ben goes to the gallows."

"But instead Ben got away. She went after him and shot his horse—and shot at you, too."

"Yes. She put us both afoot, but that's all she could do, having no experience in the woods. She didn't dare get near for fear of being recognized."

Winters took off his hat. "I can't believe that fluttery female did all that! She put on an act for us!"

"Yes, she did."

"All right. We'll go to the house tonight and get her." He put the hat on and sighed deeply. "It's goin' to be hard to get a jury to convict a woman like Miz Chartis. She'll come into court all frilled up and lookin' helpless—and they'll let her go."

Mrs. Skirrow was sitting in the office when they returned. She looked tired and glum. She shook her head. "He gone over . . ."

Reb went into the jail cell and bent over the body, feeling for a pulse. There was none. Kepler's strained muscles had relaxed and he looked peaceful in death. Mrs. Skirrow had closed his eyes; his problems were over.

Reb went back into the office and nodded to Winters, who thanked Mrs. Skirrow and walked out to the street with her.

When he came back, Winters said, "This Miz Chartis . . . she's dangerous, you figger?"

"We'd be smart to treat her as such, yes. You want me to notify Doc Bartlet to come for the body?"

"If you want." Winters sat down behind the desk and fished in a drawer for a cigar. "I 'spect the county's goin' to have to bury him. He's poor as a three-legged coyote."

"His gun might be worth ten dollars. . . ."

"That'll help some. Maybe we could auction off his boots for a dollar. . . ."

25

They waited till after dark before going to the Chartis house. Marshal Winters thought they could then be more certain of finding her in.

Howard Rankin answered the knock and opened the front door a crack. "What you want?" A very hostile snarl.

Reb put his shoulder to the door and lunged hard, knocking Rankin back across the room. He and Winters rushed in, pistols drawn. Klara Chartis was not in the room. The fireplace was blazing, and there were papers scattered in front of it. Rankin had evidently been burning them.

Reb pointed to the papers and hurried to the back of the house, hearing the back door slam. As he reached it, a shot sprang into the wood above his head.

It had come from the stable. He ducked down and went through the door, jumping into deep shadows. There was noise from the stable, a creaking as if a heavy door were opened. He ran toward the stable and was in time to see a shadowy rider burst from the stable and gallop into the dark alley.

He swore. He and Winters had walked to the house. There was no way he could go after her. . . . He stood in the alley and listened to the hoofbeats fade away. How in hell had they been warned?

He went back into the stable and scratched a match. A second horse was in one of the three stalls, a graying mare he had seen before, used to pull Klara's buggy. He shook his head; the mare might not carry him five miles.

Rankin had been burning papers—things that might be considered evidence? And Klara had been ready to shake the dust of Wakefield from her heels. They had definitely been warned. Could it have been from Mrs. Skirrow? Maybe the juicy gossip had been too much for her to keep to herself. She must have told the neighbors, never realizing its effect.

In the house he said to Winters, "She had a horse ready. She got away." He saw Rankin smirk. It annoyed him, and he grabbed Rankin and slammed him against the wall. "Where did she go?"

"I dunno! How would I know?"

"I think you know!" But he would have to beat it out of the man. He threw Rankin onto the settee. "Stay there."

Winters said, "He was burnin' letters." He held one up; it was partially charred. "This one's from Ben Kepler to Klara." He grinned. "Love letter." He sighed. "Women save them things. . . ."

"You got no call to break in here!" Rankin's voice was a growl. "I haven't done nothing."

"Your mama shot her husband, sonny," Winters said. "We hate like hell t'see that happen. And we're holdin' you till you tell us where she went."

"You can't prove anything!"

"Don't bet the farm on that, sonny."

Reb left them and walked through the house. It had two bedchambers. In the one she obviously slept in, clothes were strewn about as if in haste. A duffel bag lay on the bed, half packed, and the closet door was open. A sheen of red silk caught his eye.

He opened the door wide and stared open-mouthed at a row of gorgeous costumes, red, white, and blue silk with flashy spangles and sashes. On the shelf above were equally fancy hats with long feathers.

Behind the costumes was a poster fastened to the wall. He pushed the gaudy costumes aside and blinked in astonishment at the poster! Huge letters proclaimed CORA REED, *Star of the Show*. Other gilt letters read: *Trick Shot Artist*!

The girl in the poster was holding two smoking pistols.

The name was Cora Reed—but the face in the poster was Klara Chartis!

"Jesus!" Reb said, awed. "Trick shot artist!" That explained the incident in the store. She was an expert with guns! No wonder Kepler had been afraid of her!

And as he stared at the costumes, he recalled that Ben Kepler had worked for a time for a Wild West show. That was undoubtedly where he had met Klara! She was performing in the show! They had never married, but had carried on a long-term affair.

Until she met Homer Chartis . . . who had much more money than Kepler.

And before she became infatuated with the handsome Joe Aiken, manager of her husband's store.

Marshal Winters had the lanky Rankin on his belly on the settee, hands and feet bound, when Reb beckoned to him. "Come and see what I found."

He showed Winters the costumes and posters.

The marshal was amazed, eyes popping. "She was a circus performer!"

"Probably a Wild West show. Remember, Ben Kepler worked for one years ago. That's where they met."

"That's right! So she's a trick shot artist! I can't hardly believe it!"

"Believe it—look at that face. She changed her name, but not the face."

Winters took off his hat and sighed. "She fooled ever'-body!" He put the hat on again. "All right. I'll lock up this here house and put Rankin in a cage. Maybe he'll talk before lawyer Lisser gets him out. Could we hold him on guilty knowledge, you figger?"

"You can try."

"It'll be hard to prove what he knew . . . but his mama is facin' the rope."

"If we catch her," Reb said.

Among the partially burned papers Winters had rescued from the flames was a map with the name of a town circled in pencil. Kingston. It was on the river, probably a hundred miles east of Dyer.

Reb headed for it in the early morning. It was their only bet, since Rankin refused to open his mouth except to demand a lawyer.

Reb had no doubt that Klara and her son had agreed on a place to meet—and possibly Kingston was the first step. They could get a boat there and go downriver to—anywhere.

If they had heard Mrs. Skirrow's gossip, and it must have been the reason they were packing, they'd have had to make plans in a hurry. Maybe they had decided that Rankin would stay behind, and perhaps even sell the store and house and all the property they owned. It would bring a very tidy sum. Then he would join her.

Was there a better plan? He could not think of one.

Dyer was a tiny place, built up about an army fort that had long since been abandoned. The barracks buildings were now occupied by squatters.

Reb dismounted and talked to a few of the oldsters sitting in the mealy sunlight in front of the Alamo Saloon. They had seen a rider come through town early in the morning. When he asked them if it had been a woman, they were surprised at the question. It had not occurred to them; the rider had been wearing jeans, a shirt, coat, and hat, and been riding astride. Of course, one said, the light was poor at the time.

And whoever it had been was in a hurry.

Reb thanked them and went on. Klara was not a big woman, and, wearing men's duds, could probably pass herself off as a male if the inspection were not too close.

She had a long head start and all the advantages but one. She did not know for sure that he was on her trail. She might suppose that someone would be, but she was certainly not an experienced owlhoot.

Klara arrived in Kingston at night and went directly to the waterfront. A long stretch of riverbank, well out of the current, had been shored up by pilings and logs so that river craft could tie up stem and stern.

She got down and walked along the tethered boats, leading the horse. The *Alma* was tied just beyond a short pier, J. T. Mason had said in his letter.

And it was. Wrapping the reins around a pole, she climbed down into the boat and stamped her feet on the deck. In a moment Mason's head appeared in the companionway.

"Who's 'at?"

"It's me," she said.

He peered at her in the gloom. "Wal, damn if it ain't! I din't expect you fer a week'r more. Come on down."

He held up a candle as she entered the cluttered cabin. "You come alone?"

She nodded. "Rankin will be along later. Can you get rid of my horse?"

"Sure. I'll sell it in the mornin'."

"Don't bother with selling it. Just turn it loose away from the waterfront."

"Sure. Whatever you say."

Mason was an old-timer, skinny and spry. He had inherited the boat and had spent years in the smuggling and whiskey-running trades. Before that he had worked in the same Wild West show with Klara—who called herself Cora Reed then.

He said, "When we leavin'?"

"We have to wait for Rankin. There're papers I have to sign. The lawyer will get him out in a day'r two, and he'll come here. I'll meet him at the hotel."

The boat had only one long cabin; there were four narrow bunks and a cramped walkway. She made sure that Mason saw her pistol before she climbed into a top bunk. She was not disturbed.

In the morning Mason took the horse across town and, ignoring her instructions, sold it and the saddle to a liveryman, pocketing the money. It was damn foolish not to, he told himself. And she would never know.

* * *

Reb came to Kingston in the middle of the day. It was a village built up around an east-west road and a ferry, though the main business of the menfolk was fishing, according to the number of fishing craft tied up along the shoreline and the several short piers jutting into slack brown water. On the bank men worked at boats, some upside down on props, or repaired nets. None of them had seen a woman on a horse.

There was a wide street at right angles to the river, and around the town were houses and huts, sheds, barns, and tents. Klara could be in any one of them—if she were still here.

Reb went first to the livery stable. Liverymen were notorious for knowing all the gossip of a town. He talked to a middle-aged man with a huge potbelly. Had he seen a woman on a horse that had traveled hard?

The man shook his head. "We don't see many folks comin' along the road. I shore didn't see a woman."

"This was a woman alone."

" 'Specially no woman alone." The liveryman frowned. "I never seed a woman travelin' alone nowhere. Not ever."

Reb nodded and turned away. "Thanks."

The man said, "A horse that's traveled hard?"

"Yes?"

"I jus' bought me one."

Reb smiled. "Who from?"

"Feller name of J. T. Mason. Fisherman." The liveryman nodded toward the river. "Owns a boat called *Alma*."

"A fisherman with a horse?"

"Said a feller owed him money and paid him with the horse."

"I think he's the one I want to see."

"You'll find 'im down there—less'n he's out with the boat."

"Thanks."

It made sense, he thought, Klara going aboard a boat. She could then go downriver to the Big Muddy and on to the Mississippi. And if she got that far, he would probably never see her again.

She had fled Wakefield, so she knew the jig was up. Her house would be searched and her costumes and posters found, and possibly other evidence they had not yet discovered.

One thing she had in her favor was her son, Rankin. He was not involved in the murders. He would probably sell or arrange through lawyer Lisser to sell all their property, since she could never go back to the territory.

That done, he would go to meet her. And nothing they could do about it. Well, with a little luck Rankin might lead him to Klara. . . .

Because if Klara was on the boat, she never showed herself. Maybe he was wrong about her going aboard it. Or maybe this man, Mason, had taken her across the river and she was now far away.

But if so, why had he sold her horse?

He debated with himself about boarding the boat to look for her. If she were on the boat, it might be his last act. She was an expert with pistols, and she would have the advantage. . . .

If his theory about Klara was right, Rankin would show up here. If she were on the boat waiting for him.

If. A lot of ifs.

He kept a watch on the boat from various places and saw the fisherman, Mason, go about his regular chores. But he did not take the boat out. Others went out and came back with catches, but Mason did not move. Days went by. The boat, *Alma*, was a dirty, rusting hulk with a single mast and jib. It had a small deck structure, the deck itself strewn with lines and tackle. *Was* Klara aboard?

Reb slept in fits during the days and crept closer at night, hoping to see Rankin appear. But he did not. He ate beans from cans and tried to stay awake. He kept his horse nearby, never knowing what to expect. . . .

He nearly missed seeing the shadow that detached itself from the boat and slipped ashore. Was it Klara? Impossible to tell. The shadow hurried into the darkened town, and Reb followed, leading the horse. But the shadow disappeared.

He swore, prowling the street from one end to the other.

It was the middle of the week, and every store closed early except the two saloons. He looked in each one. They had few customers.

Pausing in front of the hotel, he frowned at the sign: COMMERICAL HOTEL, *K. Cullen Prop*. If it was Klara he followed, would she go into the hotel? Maybe she was meeting her son here. It would be easier to tell him to go to the hotel than to search the riverfront for a boat . . . at night.

The front door was three steps up from the street. Reb opened the door and was in a tiny square room. A desk took up half the space, a stairway to one side led up. An older man was nearly asleep behind the desk, sitting in an armchair, his feet propped up.

Reb leaned over the desk to shake him awake—when he heard the shot.

It had come from upstairs. One single shot, sounding muffled. Pulling the .44, Reb went up the steps. The upper hall was dim. A lantern hung on a wire at the top of the stairs, giving a reluctant yellow light. At the far end of the hallway was an open window, probably fifty feet away.

Where had the shot come from?

Reb walked slowly down the hall. Several of the doors were standing open, no one inside. He could hear snores coming from other rooms.

Light was streaming from the last room, the door slightly ajar. Pulling back the hammer of the .44, he pushed the door open wide.

The room was small, a bed to the right, a chair, and a washstand. A man was flopped facedown on the bed, his face in a bloody pool. He had been shot in the back of the head. There was a pillow on the floor with heavy powder marks on it. The bullet had gone through the pillow to deaden the sound.

Just as in the two Wakefield murders.

Reb looked out along the hall. The shot had disturbed no one. He closed the door and turned the victim's head. It was Howard Rankin!

Had Klara shot him? Who else could it have been? He

recalled that Axel had said she and her son had terrible quarrels in the store office. Was she so far gone that she was solving her problems with a gun? A gun had once brought her fame. . . .

He went out to the back window. It had a ladder nailed to the outside wall as a fire escape. She had climbed down only minutes ago. Reb swung his leg over and went down quickly, to find himself in a dark, shadowy yard with a line of privies waiting silently.

Where had she gone? She had no horse, unless she stole one. He ran around the building to the street. There were a half-dozen horses standing at hitch racks; she might have taken any one of them.

Mounting, he rode to the south end of town. It was getting light in the east; dawn would soon be here. Was that a rider in the distance? Reb spurred that way.

But the distant rider was not galloping away. The horse slowed to a walk in a wide meadow, and as Reb came close, he saw the someone wore dark clothes and no hat. It was Klara!

Reb reined in and sat, astonished. Klara was riding in a wide circle, arms raised as if acknowledging the plaudits of a crowd! She had a six-gun in either hand and began to fire shots into the air in a measured time. . . .

He stared at her. She was in an arena again, the center of attention, Cora Reed, the trick shot artist, star of the show! She bowed and waved her arms, holstering the pistols, a big smile on her face.

Reb rode slowly out to meet her. "Wonderful, Miss Reed! You've stopped the show again!"

She smiled and waved, and he slipped the pistols from her, shoving them into his belt.

Then he took her back to town.

Fawcett Rounds up

The Best of The West

Available at your bookstore or use this coupon.

___**HANGMAN'S LEGACY,** Frederic Bean	**14853**	**$3.99**
___**KILLING SEASON,** Frederic Bean	**14781**	**$3.99**
___**OUTLAW'S JUSTICE,** A.J. Arnold	**14805**	**$3.99**
___**THE GOLDEN CHANCE,** T.V. Olsen	**14803**	**$3.99**
___**THE WETHERBYS,** G. Clifton Wisler	**14830**	**$3.99**

FAWCETT MAIL SALES
400 Hahn Road, Westminster, MD 21157

Please send me the FAWCETT BOOKS I have checked above. I am enclosing $ . . . . (Add $2.00 to cover postage and handling for the first book and 50¢ each additional book. Please include appropriate state sales tax.) Send check or money order—no cash or C.O.D.'s please. To order by phone, call 1-800-733-3000. Prices are subject to change without notice. Valid in U.S. only. All orders are subject to availability of books.

Name______________________________

Address______________________________

City______________________State__________Zip__________

07 Allow at least 4 weeks for delivery. **8/92** **TAF-201**